SANCTUARY HALL

A TWISTING WORLD TALE

FINDERS & BINDERS
BOOK ONE

ALEA HENLE

CONTENT WARNING

Includes references to parental abandonment, abusive relationships, captivity, forced labor, ableism, mental illness, asylums, racism, and sexism.

PART ONE
AUGUSTA DEYO

CHAPTER I

CHANGE

Augusta Deyo's world cracked wide open seven years after the first fissure.

The rupture started at the breakfast table, no less, right after she'd swallowed warm tea well-laced with clover honey. The comfortable clothes she'd donned earlier suddenly turned too tight, from her foundation garments to her starched ivory blouse. The little lace ruffle pinned at her throat pressed against her windpipe. Even the wide legs of her plum-colored linen skirt-pants seemed to wrap close around her skin. A thin layer of sweat slicked her bobbed curls against her skull, despite the early summer morning cool. Her whole body flushed to the point that her pale hands appeared ruddy against the fussy yellow-swirls-on-cream tablecloth.

Silence drowned all the usual sounds. No more chimes of silver-plated utensils against china or grunts as her father and brothers ate. No thumps overhead where the two-months-new hired help was making beds, or clanging from the cook-housekeeper back in the kitchen No rattle of

3

wagons outside or calls from the newspaper girl parading down the street.

Even her own breathing stilled in her ears, though her throat and chest rose and fell against the taut fabric of her clothes. For that matter, everyone else in the room stopped moving and went quiet, the four of them unevenly spaced around the table that could fit twice as many with ease. The table that still had four empty chairs, including one at the foot, though no one had sat in them for years.

Seven years.

The room had barely changed a whit since then. The same yellow- and red-striped paper bedecked the walls. No one had moved the quiet landscape prints hanging at regular intervals around the room, save to dust the frames. The rectangular maple table rested atop the old woven-straw rug. The legs pressed against the exact same spots as they always had, the better to hide the worn holes revealed in the recent spring cleaning.

Had the world frozen? Albany was built on fixed land that moved only as allowed. The city had been solid for centuries, ever since the first Europeans came and bound the earth, or maybe even before when the Haudenosaunee and Mohican met and traded in the area. Not even so much as a decorative boulder in the Capitol Park dared roll a meter or two without magical permission. All the bindings that kept the city running remained as they should be. No city in the Reconstituted Union of North America could claim more solid a foundation.

Only once had Augusta felt the least quiver of land energy, that day when something in her had connected with the deep earth and found flares of hot liquid beneath the bedrock. The merest drop of the flowing power had burned, offering a hard reminder that everything in the world could move, would move, *did* move, even if slower than humans noticed.

Everything moved sooner or later.

Everything changed.

Including her, whether or not she liked it.

Seven years ago, she'd hovered on the brink between girl and woman. She'd matured into a capable woman in her early twenties, trying to walk in her mother's footsteps and finding them—still—always—too big.

The lukewarm tea tasted of bile as she swallowed. Lifting a shaky hand to her throat, she tore open the lace ruffle. The small circle brooch that had kept it closed popped open, and the pin scratched but didn't draw blood.

The brooch slipped through her fingers and clattered as it came to rest against the edge of her plate. Sound and movement returned—wagon wheels rumbled outside, thuds overhead, and harsh breaths echoed around the table.

Across from Augusta, her older brother, Jacob Deyo crunched on a bite of buttered toast. He dropped the half-eaten crust onto his plate alongside congealing eggs of an appallingly cheery yellow. He had their father's solid build and dark-brown hair, gelled flat against his head, and wore a perfectly creased gray suit of summerweight wool with a wine-red tie in a loose bow and a matching handkerchief folded in the top right breast pocket. Yet the wide brown eyes in the stark, lean lines of his face spoke of their mother's blood.

Her father, Cornelius Deyo, wore a more sedate blue suit than his son in an older, classic cut, his collar and cuffs stark white against his ruddy-beige coloring. He folded his napkin and set it alongside his plate. The eggs and toast were scattered over the surface, hiding how much or little he'd eaten other than consuming all of his slices of bacon. The end of his long, thin nose twitched, but otherwise the muscles of his broad face were taut, and the white at his temples stark against his brown hair.

Only her youngest brother, Danny, continued to eat as though nothing had happened. His flat cap hung off one side of his chair, clean and neat but a bit battered and thus a good match for his shirt and breeches, the latter held up by blue suspenders. He slipped a sixth piece of bacon from the serving platter and munched on. His eyes—a lighter brown than father or brother—flashed Augusta's way to see if she'd make a fuss.

Not today, not with their father's words still echoing in her head.

Not when she still held hope she'd misheard him.

"Would you mind repeating that?" Jake—not Jakey anymore, even among family—raised his eyebrows as he leaned back in his chair, the wood creaking beneath him. He braced his hands against the edge of the table, fingers creasing the linen.

At least Augusta wasn't the only one taken aback. Small comfort, but she'd learned to take it where she could get it.

"It's been seven years since your mother left. There's been no sign of her since. No letters, no cards with blurry postmarks, not even any sightings in responses to the notices I placed in newspapers throughout the country." Father rubbed his forehead, gaze fixed on the table. "I wish this weren't so, but . . . under the circumstances, I'm petitioning to have her declared legally dead."

Danny hadn't seemed to pay attention, but he shot to his feet. His chair creaked and lurched back, nearly hitting the wall. Crumbs of bacon dropped from his clenched hands as he asked, voice high and tight, "Mama's dead? Frank and Callie, too? Cousin Nanette?"

"No, no." Their father rose, leaning over the table to take Danny's hands between his. "As far as I know they're all alive. But there's been no word of any of them. Or *from* them, and Frank and Callie are old enough they should remember our address and be able to send word."

Augusta ran a finger along the top of the empty chair next to her, where her younger sister had once sat. Another empty beyond it had been last used by their distant cousin Nanette. Across the way, Frank's chair sat empty between Jake and Danny, and their mother's at the foot of the table.

"They're not coming home? Ever?" Danny's round face looked older than his years, and for the first time his voice cracked.

"I don't know. I'll never stop looking for them, posting advertisements, paying investigators, searching for the kind of pathwalker who could locate them." Father squeezed Danny's hands, but his shoulder rounded and the lines of his face spoke of exhaustion. "Maybe someday . . ."

"But it's been years." Jake snatched a piece of bacon and crumbled it over his plate. "Anything could have happened." He leaned over to rub Danny's back. "We're still here, same as always. How much do you even remember Frank or Callie? You were little when they left."

"Frank used to get breezes to steal my toys and hide them up high, then Callie would get them back for me." Danny stuck his chin out. "It was a game between them. And Nanette sang me to sleep, never using words only *la la la.*"

"It's just Mother who Father's asking to have declared dead." Augusta tried to smile at Danny as she forced the words out. "Seven the years to the day since she left. You couldn't wait another week or month or . . ." Her voice cracked too, and she swallowed hard.

"The longer I wait the more difficult it will be." Father let go of Danny and stood tall, shoulders back as he gestured at the room. "We cannot go on as we are."

Another long silence, but this time only voices went quiet. The creaks and thuds of the house and neighborhood remained. Danny settled back in his chair but didn't scoot it forward. He kicked the legs, flat soles hitting hard against the wood.

Jake had his hands in his lap, twiddling his thumbs.

"You want to remarry." Augusta lifted her chin high to stare at her father, hands clenched.

Her father opened his mouth, shut it, then turned his hands out and nodded. "Yes."

"Have you already chosen . . ." She couldn't say *a new wife*. The words stuck in her throat.

"There's . . . there may be someone, but I haven't said anything. I don't have the right, yet." All at once, his face seemed less lined than before, as though he'd doffed a great load. "I will introduce you if I may, when the time is right. But for now, if you'll excuse me, I have an appointment with a lawyer."

Finality filled his voice, the kind of note that Augusta had learned not to challenge but wait to try another way and another time, understanding even that might fail. Her mother had taught her that. Nevertheless, their father circled the table to give each of them a personal farewell.

A pat on the head for Danny and warning not to be late for his session with the Kanien'kéha tutor in the afternoon.

A handshake for Jake, and similar advice, but instead of the school Jake would head for the Whistle Institute where father and son both worked as scientists and administrators.

So too did Augusta labor there, in a variety of capacities. Sometimes she served as a research subject, much as her mother had before her, although Augusta's magic came from her father's side.

"I'm sorry." Her father's arms were gentle and firm as he gave her a brisk hug. "See you at work?"

Then he was gone without waiting for an answer, assuming her assent.

"Let me walk with you!" Danny lurched from the table, shoes pounding against the floor and sending vibrations through the rug and boards.

Augusta's teeth rattled and chattered because of Danny.

No, because she trembled. She huddled in place, arms wrapped across her chest. The slats of the chair back creaked and shifted as she rocked and shivered. So cold. Tears trickled down her face, leaving warm tracks.

Mother gone seven years without a word.

Dead or as good as.

Soon to be official.

"Don't." Jake bent and rested warm hands on her shoulders, though his fingers shook. "Gussie . . ."

The old nickname didn't trigger her usual instinctive glare and snarl for once. He'd stopped calling her that— everyone in the family had—after her mother had left. If anything, being Gussie for a moment gave her a bit of the old days *before* back.

He pulled her out of her chair and held her close. A few teardrops fell on her shoulders, maybe more on her hair, but his chin was firm where it pressed against her temple.

The two of them held each other. Steadied. Warmed.

Jake pulled back first.

"Father's right, you know. We can't live this way forever." He waved at the wallpaper, the chairs carefully arranged around the table, half showing signs of use but others nearly as new as the day Mother had re-covered them with needlework of her own making. Each cushion bore a bird chosen specifically for its usual occupant. A majestic snowy owl for Father and keen-eyed kestrel for Jake. A bobolink for Danny. For Augusta, a northern cardinal with vivid red accents to the female's brownish-tan markings.

"We haven't done so bad." Augusta brushed the detailed osprey with a wide wingspan that covered her mother's seat cushion.

"Nothing's changed since that day."

"Nothing?" Augusta waved at their clothes.

"You wear the same styles and colors as Mother instead of the girl's outfits you used to." He smoothed a hand over the sharp lines of his suit. "And you'd have me dressed same as Father if I didn't order my own clothes."

Too true. She dressed much as her mother had except far less jewelry. Augusta never wore anything more than a modest pin. She scooped the plain silver circle from the table and refastened the lace ruffle at her throat.

"We can't stay like this., Jake repeated.

Why not? But the words stuck in her throat.

He hugged her again, then pulled away, wiping his face with the back of a hand. Blushed lightly when she nodded at the exquisitely folded kerchief still tucked in his pocket, though he didn't remove it.

"Walk with me to work?" he asked.

She swallowed, voice hoarse as she managed a level reply. "Give me a moment."

"I'll wait at the door. Five minutes, no less, and the count starts now."

She waited through the vibrations of his passage out and along the hall, then lifted both hands. Stroked her bare fingers and wrists, tugged on unbedecked ears, and traced a curve over her thin bosom where a necklace would hang, if she ever wore one.

Her mother had taken all the jewelry in the house with her. She'd even dug into Augusta's bureau and removed the small string of pearl beads, a bequest from Augusta's paternal grandmother. Mother had taken every small item of material value in the house down to the solid silverware given at her wedding and used only on the most festive occasions.

She'd also taken her middle son and younger daughter and a distant cousin only a few years older than Augusta, but abandoned the rest of the family.

Left Augusta to wonder why.

CHAPTER 2

FAMILIAR PLACES

For all Jake's fine words about change, no sooner had he adjusted the angle of his straw boater hat than he headed off on the same route to work as always.

Augusta tucked a gloved hand through the crook of his arm, fingers pressing lightly against the soft wool. A small, peaked cap perched atop her head, offering no shade against the warm sunlight pouring down. Her tan duster covered her clothes from neck to ankle, the lightweight fabric rising and twisting in the breeze. All the same, her sensible leather shoes and the hems of her skirt-pants gathered a fine layer of dust because it hadn't rained recently and the sidewalks were filthy save where residents or their servants scrubbed them down.

The new concrete street gleamed gray in the sunlight. Blurry wheel marks lined the center of the narrow expanse, which barely had room for two carriages to pass. Town-houses lined either side, most four-story brick affairs with one or two shorter, squatter homes. Some of their cousins on their father's side turned up their noses at the humdrum neighborhood, but Augusta appreciated the several trees growing along the sidewalk offering cool shade, rustling leaves, and even a whiff of lilacs from purple blooms across the way. So much nicer than the barren streetscapes around the newest outside-of-town mansions.

The houses here had been in place long enough to have a solid feel, although the earth under the street hadn't quite adjusted to the new concrete. The fixedness was less, but present, as stone and metal shaped by human hands worked as well as magic to make earth and plants keep still. Some politicians and businessmen grumbled that laying worked stone and metal was better than paying binders to ensure the land didn't move, because binding spells required value be given as well as received, and needed regular tending. But surely that was only because those who spoke against binders rarely had any magic themselves. They'd never experienced the glory of making a balanced binding or been driven by shared pain to release a captive elemental.

Then again, Augusta had binding magic and might be a wee bit biased.

Overall, everything in the neighborhood was in its place and the bindings balanced. Only a few points of movement flickered against Augusta's awareness. A rosebush in the small side yard at the corner busily turned around to give more of its leaves a chance to absorb sun. The lamppost at the intersection with a wider street slowly shifted to center itself in the sidewalk.

A looming gray in the sky and a tang to the air suggested a storm on the way. The breeze flowing east carried a hint of voices and syllables as it zipped by. If

Mother, Frank, or Callie were there, they might have shared what news the air spirits carried, for all three could speak with air elementals.

But they weren't present. That was the whole point of Father's morning announcement.

Augusta's free hand tightened around the wooden handle of her umbrella. A growing ache in her knuckles forced her to ease her grip.

At least taking the usual route to work required little in the way of effort on her part. A wave here, a nod there, perhaps a small smile when the youngest Sullivan escaped through the front door of his home covered in nothing but suds, bright white against his fawn skin, and raced down the street before being recaptured with much giggling by his fully clad but decidedly damp third-oldest sister.

Further down, two girls Danny's age with light-brown skin and dozens of bead-tipped braids skipped along the street swinging a covered basket between them. Madame Marignan, their mother, strolled slower and called after them in French, reminding them not to race and to behave as proper young ladies and not unruly horses. The meaning came through, although Madame Marignan came from Martinique and used words and phrases Augusta had never heard among her French-speaking relatives.

Jake snorted. She turned his way only to choke on a mouthful of dust.

A couple of autowagons chugged past, kicking up whirls in their wake. Both were newish, with gleaming sides—black for one and yellow the other—and bright, crisp canopy tops. Several people walking to work or the stores on the other side of the street also coughed as the wagons passed.

The black had a thin trail of steam from the exhaust pipe at the back, thick with as much moisture as the impending storm. A water spirit whirled in loops through the engine, propelling the long vehicle forward. Augusta lacked the magic to speak with the spirit the way speakers could, but couldn't miss how the binding that kept the spirit within the wagon glowed with health and reciprocity.

The people riding the autowagons matched, their light-brown skin bearing highlights from taupe to russet. Mostly men in gray or brown European-style suits as fine as Jake's, but adorned with quillwork fringe. Feathers adorned their caps, three black and white feathers rising high above each head. No doubt Haudenosaunee come to the city, likely from nearby Kanièn:ke.

One of the men nodded at Augusta and Jake as they motored past. He smiled as he patted the damp tank at the center-back of the wagon, the focal point of the binding between element and machine.

That wagon chugged far down the street before taking a turn and stopping in front of an old, ornate brick mansion at the corner, while the other wagon continued along the street. Jake's muscles tensed under her fingers, easily felt despite the layers of glove and clothes. Both could tell, despite the distance, that one of the men hopped off the wagon and marched up through a wrought-iron fence to the front door of the Whistle Institute.

No one answered the door. If Augusta were closer, she'd have called out that it was too early. The clock had yet to ring out the hour. The man must have figured out the door wouldn't open, for he turned around and rejoined his fellows, and the wagon headed off and away.

"Had you heard of visitors being expected?" She quickened her pace, Jake needing no encouragement to match her.

A diversion would be lovely. Something utterly unrelated to the business her father was conducting elsewhere in the city, and thus capable of distracting her from that.

"No." Jake frowned, then emitted a huff. "Though old George was complaining the other day about official letters from the Kanien'kehá:ka demanding some new accommodation or other. He didn't say what."

"Don't let Father catch you calling George old." Augusta lifted her hand from her brother's arm long enough to wag a finger at his reference to their father's cousin, George Whistle IV. "He's two years younger than Father."

"Two years, five months, and three days."

"And they both know it," Augusta joined Jake to say together. The friendly rivalry between the cousins and their children was old, familiar, and comfortable.

But not worth distracting from the earlier sight, or the news that Jake had heard something of the matter.

"No one told me anyone might come calling. Are they donors? Scientists? Do we give them the usual tour?" Everyone who worked at the Institute or was affiliated with it for very long learned how to show visitors around, ideally encouraging a liberality of funds to help support the scientific exploration of the how and why of magic.

"Well, check first to see if Father or George wants to see them, before taking them around."

"Of course." Augusta sighed, but lashing back that she didn't need the reminder wasn't worth the hassle.

Another autowagon powering along distracted her. The long red-and-black beast boasted a sail fluttering above the canopy, with a stout breeze puffing away. A young fair-skinned man in a flat cap drove, while two older men in fine gray suits sat in the back puffing on cigars.

The smoke was worse than the steam from the water-powered autowagon—but couldn't hide the pain and desperation emanating from the magic binding the air elemental, practically a sulfuric miasma. Augusta pulled away from Jake and covered her nose and mouth.

Her brother quirked an eyebrow at her but made no sign of noticing the elemental's distress. Then again, he resembled the vast majority of the population—by her father and the other Institute scientists' count—in having little to no magic. At best, most had enough binding power to set a garden and keep the plants from wandering off, and nothing more.

Augusta had more, though she was only a middling binder or unbinder—she'd met too many with far more strength to have any illusions about the extent of her gift. Still, she possessed enough power to tweak a captive binding a time or five so that the bound elemental might escape. She hadn't even minded the fuss the one instance when she'd gotten caught out as responsible. She was registered with the Institute, after all, with the acknowl-edged rights and responsibilities under the laws of the Reconstituted Union to tend the deals between humans and the elements and undo any that were clearly abusive.

The first time she'd done it, as a budding twelve-year old, her mother had given her a hug and treat after. Her father had patted her head, then argued with her mother about how old Augusta needed to be before she could come to the Institute for testing.

Augusta didn't remember who'd won, only the hundreds of lessons her father had given her over the years on how to undo bindings. She had a knack for it, he'd said more than once, and should use that and leave binding to those who weren't so good at undoing.

Equally, Augusta remembered her mother's pleasure every time Augusta freed a spirit.

Before the wind-powered autowagon moved too far away, she hooked a finger in the magic that kept the spirit imprisoned and laboring hard. The binding stretched, as pliable as taffy—but even sweet masses of boiled sugar and butter had a limit to how far they could lengthen before they broke.

She held firm, settling back on her heels as she resisted the pull to let go. This was the third captive element powering an autowagon that she'd freed in a week, and they got easier all the time. Besides, magic fluttered along her skin, silky pleasure akin to petting a cat or dog.

The bond snapped. The autowagon slowed, people in it grousing and scratching their heads as it rolled to a stop several blocks down.

"What did you . . ." Jake squinted at the distant mess.

The air spirit soared free. It whisked back to twirl around Augusta—at least, she assumed it was the same elemental—before pushing Jake's hat from his head and making him chase it for several steps.

Augusta continued without him, passing by the street that led to the front door of the Institute in favor of the narrower, shadier entry around back. Going in the front, past the discreet sign that marked the Institute as a charitable, scientific endeavor planted amidst a cluster of mansions, meant dealing with the intricate locks attached to the immense doors.

This, too, was familiar. Unchanging. She only went in the front way on festive occasions when the Institute made all effort to attract monied patrons.

Mother had worked at the Institute alongside Father before she left—not every day, but often. Augusta hadn't helped much, as she'd still attended the nearby girl's school. But within a few years, she'd started as an assistant and ever since, it had become part of what didn't change in her life. She wore the same kind of clothes as always—so did Jake for all his airs and occasional dandyisms—and did the same kind of tasks as their mother.

Augusta paused halfway down the stairs to the back entrance, staring at the simple wooden door set within a broad stone arch. How long she didn't know, only that Jake recaptured his hat and caught up.

"What's wrong?" He set a warm hand against her upper back, his chest heaving and forehead shining with sweat.

"Mother was here." How could Augusta not think about her, and how much she followed in Mother's steps, especially with the morning's sharp reminder?

"Of course she was. She and Father met at the Institute, right after he founded it."

"Not then, right before she left. That day, or a day before at most. I think. Maybe." Augusta closed her eyes, trying to summon up memories—and failing. So much of time right before her mother's departure was a blurry blank.

"Oh." Jake frowned, then shrugged. "We were short a matron, then, I think."

"Do you remember?" Her breath caught in her throat, for he sounded as unclear as her.

"I'd just graduated college and started working here, which was a lot different than I'd expected, I tell you." He pressed against her back, urging her down the stairs. "What does it matter, it's years ago."

"She didn't take me." The words escaped Augusta

before she could call them back, so plaintive and high and almost childish in tone.

Jake whirled, pulling her in to lean against the cool, shaded door. The mingled pity and pain on his face made clear he understood which day she meant.

It wasn't something she'd have mentioned if she'd had a second to think. She did her crying at night when she cried anymore, in the dark, when she could bury her face against the sheets and hope that someday the tears would ease the hurt. Better that way. Father and Jake's faces had been gray with strain and hurt themselves, those first days, and Danny had wept and yelled and thrown things enough for all of them.

"You wanted to go?" Jake grabbed her hand, staring straight at her.

"How could I know? I didn't have the chance to think about it." Augusta tugged free, fumbling as she turned away and tried to match key with hole. "I just wish she hadn't left me behind."

"But . . . didn't you choose?" His breath was hot against her neck.

"Choose?"

"When she asked. I wouldn't leave Father alone, though I . . ."

Augusta whirled around, her turn to stare at him. To study and note the twitch in his cheek, pulse throb at his temple, and working of his throat.

"She asked you? To go with her?" That he'd stayed didn't surprise her. He'd always been closer to their father than their mother. But that their mother had asked *him* . . .

"Didn't she ask you?" His voice dropped so low she barely heard it, but couldn't miss the surprise on his face.

"I don't remember." Pain rippled through her, blocking

her throat until she swallowed hard. A bitter tang bloomed in her mouth. "I don't remember her asking. I don't remember anything of when she left. Just dinner the night before, when she was shivering and her hand shook so much she could barely eat—and then the morning the day after, when she was gone."

CHAPTER 3

POWERS AND PROBLEMS

hy weep when Augusta could lose herself in work instead? Jump right into the comfort of everyday labor and decision-making.

The hinges creaked as the heavy back door swung open. Escaping Jake's awkward pats on her back, she marched in. Her nose wrinkled at the lingering dampness in the air. That wasn't usual. It *should* smell freshly cleaned, for the tiled floor bore signs of recent mopping. The white-washed walls were mostly clean, and the few finger marks marring the side wall were watery and likely to leave little residue when they dried.

The room itself was nothing more than a simple rectangle with only a narrow, scarred table along one wall for furniture. Doors to either side led to closets and pantries and stairs, while the far end led to the kitchens and laundry and other work spaces that hadn't changed much when the building went from being a family residence to a place of scientific inquiry—or so Augusta's father often averred.

Her mother had once sniffed and said that was because he didn't spend much time below the stairs. She'd never explained, and Augusta could only guess what she meant, since the Institute required a sizable number of servants to handle cooking, cleaning, and the endless piles of laundry, not to mention watching over the research subjects in residence.

Jake's pats turned into a fumbling attempt to remove her duster. She turned, letting him help her once she'd pulled off her gloves and tucked them in a pocket. Her hat she removed on her own and gave to him to put in the closet with his boater. Several light coats hung there already, the same with hats, many of which she recognized as belonging to the people who should be here.

She welcomed any sign of normalcy.

"I'm off and up." Jake gave her one last pat, and then a sour look when she turned around and rose on tiptoes to pat the top of his head in the same manner. "Time to hit the books and see where we can cut corners. Father warned me there'd be a lot to do when he offered the job, but I don't think even he realized how dam—dashed expensive this place is. Don't spend money we haven't got on new linens."

"That's not what I do." Her weak words echoed back at her from the bare walls, lost under the clomp of him speeding up to the second floor. Though he knew that, even if he didn't appreciate exactly what she did.

Which made him no different than anyone else, including her.

Jake had graduated from college and plunged directly into the twin hearts of the Institute: scientific inquiry and the finances that allowed the scientists to conduct their investigations. His work was complicated and required detailed attention, of course, as the Institute stumbled along with an ever-shifting mixture of reliance on funding from the state and private donations, and the occasional collaboration with the institution across town studying the newfangled field of psychology.

After Augusta had finished at the local girl's school, their father had offered her a place at the Institute doing what he'd *said* her mother had and which had been sorely missed since her mother's departure. It had seemed appropriate then that she step up and become what he called the heart of the Institute, knowing just enough about what went on in every aspect to ensure supplies were ordered and received, and employee grumbles reached the right ears. She also offered tours to visitors and potential donors.

Now she wondered if this *was* what her mother had done, for Augusta had rarely set foot in the Institute until taking the position, and never seen her mother there.

Though it was certainly not coincidence that Augusta's work flitting about the whole of the mansion ensured she met all of the eligible—and some not-so-eligible—scientists who came to work for a few years before going off to labor at universities or medical establishments. None had roused any particular interest in her, and she didn't expect any ever would, but her father continued to hope, audibly.

She headed up the stairs, going slowly enough that the clomp of Jake's steps vanished into the distance before she reached the first floor. The new electric lanterns in the stairwell made it bright as day, helped by regular coats of whitewash on the walls. No fancy wallpaper or paint here; that was for the main rooms on the first floor only, where her father and the other Institute leaders entertained donors and wealthy families with members suffering the ill-effects of possessing magic. Only rarely did individuals or families enjoying the benefits of strong powers think to seek advice on how to avoid or mitigate their eventual decline and fall.

Or so Father often said.

The third floor differed completely from the first, the former servants' quarters now used to house those research subjects lacking funds to live on their own while in the care of the Institute, or whose families, unable to care for them, had entrusted them to the Institute thanks to funding from the State. Thoroughly whitewashed walls and matching ceilings and tiled floors made any flutter of color stand out—usually denoting someone in motion. Even the ankle-length cream apron female servants wore over their uniform pale-blue blouses and skirt-pants stood out against the stark white. Nevertheless, Augusta nearly ran into the woman bustling down the corridor despite the warning ripple of blue-and-cream at the top of the stairs.

Augusta stopped a hand's breadth away, grabbing hold of the doorframe rather than plowing into Mrs. O'Leary. Standing so close, she had to crick her neck back to look up at the older woman even though the house matron went two steps backward after the almost-collision. The elder's blue eyes twinkled behind a pair of silver-framed pince-nez set atop her twitchy nose. The messy bun of gray-blonde curls above her high forehead always seemed on the brink of collapsing, although it never had as far as Augusta was aware. A heavy chatelaine bearing a myriad of jangling keys hung at her waist, and she lacked the small white cap the female attendants wore, but otherwise was attired in the same uniform.

"Ah, you're here and just as well not ten minutes earlier, or you'd have seen quite the mess." Mrs. O'Leary wiped her hands on her apron. "We've a new speaker just arrived, poor dear, and she's pretty far gone. Her husband did all the speaking with her barely managing a word, though you could see clear enough she understood most of what he said."

A few thin puddles filled lines of grout around damp tiles. Likewise, a few breezes played chase down the hall.

"At a guess she's strong at speaking with water spirits?" Augusta asked.

"You'd be right, but not just water. She speaks to air, too, at least a little, and has a breeze or two blowing rain about her though she's tried to wave it off. I've settled her at the far end of the women's ward, but we might want to put her in the little chamber up against the toilet, if I can get the help to clear enough of the odds-and-ends we've been storing there out of it first." Mrs. O'Leary frowned and pursed her lips. "Breezes inside a building are a bit much, but one can get used to them even if they do require lots of paperweights. Rain now, I'd just as soon stayed outside— so much harder to tidy up after. We've already had a bit of a squall this morning when her husband left."

"So I see." Augusta let go of the doorframe and tested the floor. A little slick, but not dangerously so.

"There's more, but perhaps not here." Mrs. O'Leary clicked her tongue and waved to a maid heading down the hall with mop and bucket as she led Augusta the other way.

Augusta caught a glimpse of the new arrival in the woman's ward—a small figure in the darker blue attire provided to residents sitting on a bed with her head in her hands, pale beige fingers bright against the dark sleeves of her dress and her bobbed black hair. A small raincloud wreathed the top of her head, twisting in a light breeze. The posture raised old memories, as Augusta's cousin Nanette had sat just that way when she first came to stay with the family.

Across the room, the other resident woman speaker

stood near the wall. Small gusts of wind wreathed around her, pulling from the water to take on a foggy gray hue.

The new speaker appeared to maybe be in her thirties. If so, she was most unusual. The longer-term resident was in her mid-twenties, which was roughly the usual age for speakers to lose themselves to the elements. Neither spoke.

Nearby, the men's ward had only one occupant—a short, thin Chinese man suffering symptoms of his powers swamping him despite being far older than usual, her father's age at least. His papers stored downstairs indicated he'd immigrated and naturalized as a citizen around the time of Augusta's birth, shortly after passage of the Global Naturalization Act. He nodded at her and his lips moved in what she took as a greeting as she passed by.

Three doors further down, Mrs. O'Leary escorted Augusta into her office. The small chamber had a window with a view of the state house in the distance. The desk was situated so as to allow anyone seated behind it to glance out the window or at someone in the wooden chair opposite. Filing cabinets in mismatched shades of gray filled most of the space.

Augusta eased around the cabinets to settle on the guest chair.

"That poor woman." Mrs. O'Leary did not sit. Arms crossed over her chest, she drummed her fingers against her upper arms. "I'm sure I'd be leaking rain if I were a water speaker and married to such a man. Was clear enough he's ready to have her committed and find himself a new wife to care for him and any children, common law or what have you, though he didn't seem so out-of-pocket as all that. I've nothing against men, mind you. I married two myself. The first was a lovable rascal who led me quite the turnabout while the second was the sweetest you'd ever find on earth, and I'll have no other after him. But no matter how much I might feel for a body eking out a living for a family and having a wife living more and more with elemental spirits and less with humans, making things harder, and maybe yes you bring her to a place such as this to care for her on the State's dollar—but you come back, day after day to visit rather than dropping her off as though she's a loaf of bread."

The torrent of words washed over Augusta. This was normal, for Mrs. O'Leary passed judgment any time someone new took up residence—and had strong opinions on families who used the Institute to take the burden of caring for their kin versus those who kept the responsibility inasmuch as their energy and funds sufficed, but sought help from the Institute.

But it was also an apt reminder for Augusta that husbands and wives carrying on after spouses were no longer able was normal too. Her father wasn't doing anything that hadn't been done before, many times. She should be grateful that her father had a chance at another marriage, even if that wasn't something she'd ever wanted for herself since the first time she realized she didn't have to wed.

And she was happy for him.

At least a little.

It was everything else that disturbed her. The steps needed for him to be free to move on, the finality of her mother's departure, and Augusta's lack of understanding of the why behind it.

She hated change—even if only now did realization dawn of just how much and at the same time how little Augusta's life had altered since her mother's departure.

She'd finished school and stepped into her mother's shoes to some degree, but otherwise?

She'd stayed still.

No longer, not with Father bent on something new.

Cold trickled down Augusta's back, as though a breeze had decided to come tease her. Not impossible, but neither was it likely. Augusta started, then refocused on Mrs. O'Leary just as the older woman shifted to practical matters.

"Elsewise, we've the two other speakers here." Mrs. O'Leary's chair creaked as she settled down, hands busy sorting papers on her desk. "The one air and the other air and earth who's most unhappy about being up this high. Mr. Zhang that is, the one the railroad engineers sent up and have been inquiring about week after week, though I've heard there are plans to take him out to the Hall later this week, since he stopped managing so much as a single word some time ago, not that anyone's told me officially."

"I'll find out." Augusta stole a piece of blank paper and a pencil and made a note, sketching out quickly other items to do for the day. "So three speakers all told. Who else is in residence?"

"One pathwalker."

"Only one?" Augusta asked.

"Jim Jackson left late last night. Said he heard something calling him and had to go. Mattie Smith's still here, though the way she's pacing her room I doubt she'll stay long." Mrs. O'Leary shrugged. "Pathwalkers do come and go fast."

Augusta nodded. "It's the nature of their magic to be always on the move."

"The curse of their magic, more like. Seems as all magics

are curses the more power you get, and the older you grow." Mrs. O'Leary gave Augusta a level glance. "Pathwalkers can't stay anywhere. Speakers get so busy talking to the elements they can't handle us humans. Binders try to nail down nearly everything around them, wanting to fix us all in place."

Augusta froze, breath catching in her throat. She was a middling strong binder—easy to know her limitations after having met the few high-powered binders who'd consulted with the Institute. She had noticed that they didn't do well with change, but hadn't considered how much that might apply to her as well.

The lack of change at home . . . had she contributed to it? Even though her father had focused on teaching her how to unbind, so she could help undo when the Institute scientists had patients practice binding under observation, she was still a binder first and foremost.

Mrs. O'Leary either hadn't noticed Augusta's stillness, or was polite enough not to show it. "Whispers say there might even be a lightfoot on the way here, and if you could find the truth of that I'd be obliged. Wherever would we put one?"

"I don't know, the same as we put everyone else—in the men's ward or women's ward or children's room." Augusta tilted her head in the direction of the rest of the floor.

"But will they stay? What do lightfeet do?" Mrs. O'Leary asked.

"I think they talk to ghosts, but I'm not sure."

"Pshaw, anyone can talk to ghosts if they've a mind." The older woman waved a dismissive hand.

"Maybe they understand when the ghosts speak back?" Augusta shrugged. It was a moot point until and unless a lightfoot actually showed up.

"I'd think that would be speakers understanding,

unless lightfeet's what they call ghost speakers?" Mrs. O'Leary sighed. "It's been near fifty years since the Troubles and the Reconstitution, and well over a hundred since the year of no summer doubled or tripled the amount of magic in the world, or whatever the scholars say. You'd think we'd know more about the ins and outs of speakers and binders and pathwalkers by now."

"That's why the Institute, and others like it, exist." Augusta folded the list of tasks and tucked it into her pocket as she rose from her chair.

"Well, they're not doing near enough a good job to help all the poor people deal with their curses." The older woman shook her head, bun teetering but not falling apart.

"If you don't think we're doing well enough, you're welcome to try yourself." The light, resonant tones had a bit of bite.

Augusta startled, having noted footsteps down the hall but thought they were the staff taking the patients down to meet with the scientists. The clatter of Mrs. O'Leary's chair legs scraping the floor indicated she was similarly surprised.

The Whistle of the Whistle Institute filled the doorway. Augusta's father's cousin George was only a few millimeters taller than Augusta and quite a bit shorter than Mrs. O'Leary, but managed to loom nevertheless. His eyes flashed in a tanned face, courtesy of many hours spent outdoors, though he had bags under his eyes suggesting problems sleeping. He resembled Augusta's father, though no doubt he'd have put it the other way around, with dark-brown hair and eyes, a long nose, and a solid build encased in a classic gray suit of the highest quality fabrics. George didn't actually have much to do with the Institute itself, preferring to live outside of town, but stopped by at least once every other month.

He gave Augusta a thin-lipped smile, but Mrs. O'Leary received a raised eyebrow.

The prime administrator of the Institute lifted her chin, rising and standing her ground. "I just think it's a pity when a woman of thirty gets so she can't talk to her husband or babies and he drops her off here with little more than a wave good-bye, and unless she's different from the dozens of speakers we've had here before, she'll live out whatever's left of her life never speaking another word to a human being."

"It is a pity," George said in a mild tone, yawning, "but we'll care for her—"

"And study her," Mrs. O'Leary said.

"And someday the insights gleaned from her and others will let us help speakers control their power. I presume you're referring to the new arrival? In which case I've come to help make the first notes and evaluate her for residence here or longer-term consignment to the Hall. I understand she speaks mostly with water elementals?" He turned, half-in and half-out of the doorway.

"Yes."

"Have her brought to the Blue Room. I'll check on the air speakers after her."

Mrs. O'Leary waited for him to clear the doorway completely before she headed off, steps solid and unmistakable as she headed down the hall.

As soon as she passed him, George turned to smile at Augusta. "And how are you today, my dear cousin?"

Augusta slipped into the hall in Mrs. O'Leary's wake, thinking back to the young woman hunched on her bed, and soon to be herded down to the second floor. "She resembles Nanette."

"Nanette?" George blinked and frowned.

"My cousin, the one who . . . left with Mother." Though the new arrival was older, her posture and attitude made Augusta uncomfortable, particularly this day. Mother had chosen to take Nanette, but not Augusta.

"Ah yes, I remember her now. A strong speaker, very strong, and with a decided preference for water. She nearly caused a flood during her first visit here. We had to replace the carpet in the great room." George sighed, glaring down as though he could see through to the room in question, two floors below. "I wanted to take her out to the Hall straightaway—the stronger speakers do better there, and cause decidedly less havoc—but your mother insisted on inspecting the Hall first, and the next thing I knew she'd gone off and taken the girl with her." He patted Augusta's shoulder. "I'm sorry if the memory—"

"That's where Mother went? To Sanctuary Hall?" A vague memory slipped through Augusta's head—of dinner the night before when Mother had returned from a journey. All the family were present plus Nanette, but there was little conversation and much tension. Nanette hadn't said more than a whispered "thank you" when passed the bread. Frank and Callie had hissed and bubbled at each other through their drinks. Father and Jake were withdrawn. And Mother sat still and cold in her seat.

Sanctuary Hall. The Whistle family home in the country, where George lived and oversaw the staff caring for those speakers who couldn't care for themselves.

"I've never been."

"If you ever decide to visit, you would be welcome."

George clapped his hands and beamed at her. "I'm taking my wife and girls there later this week. You could join us."

"Maybe I will." It might help Augusta adjust to her father's decision, even all these years later, if she only knew more about why Mother left and left her behind.

She could start by retracing her mother's steps.

CHAPTER 4

COMPETING CLAIMS

The distant clang of the doorbell woke Augusta from a seated nap in her too-comfy cushioned work chair. Her dreams melted way, leaving only surety that Mother had been there with a message. Or a request? Or, pleading for something? Had tears trickled down her cheeks?

Horrid all the way around.

The usual environs of Augusta's office provided comfort. Little change here, other than the piles of papers on the broad desk and in the filing cabinets lining one wall. Those shifted, but never shrank. The glorious wallpaper of flowering vines in purples and green delighted, as always, even if it had started to fade where the morning sun shone on it day after day.

A studio portrait of her family from *before* hung on the opposite wall, where the sun never touched it. Mother and Father seated at the center, with all five children arrayed around. Everyone smiling.

The doorbell rang again. Someone should open it. At

least seven people had offices closer. Augusta got up anyway. Her feet wavered and she grabbed the edge of the desk, nearly pitching it against the plain wooden chair for guests on the other side. Pins-and-needles aches ran along her legs for a few moments, then dissipated. She adjusted the fall of her blouse and the lace at her throat. Pant hems swishing around her ankles, she stalked around the desk and out of the office.

A half-dozen or more other footsteps drowned out hers.

No need to go down and open the doors. They were spread wide and letting quite a warm draft in. She leaned against the railing and peered down from the oval balcony at the swooping stairway and the wide hall below. Across the way, Jake and several of the scientists did likewise, and farther along a few servants. Always good to have company when peeping down at guests.

Warm, harsh afternoon sunlight mixed with the orange glow of the brass lamps lining the walls and glinting off the bits of gold leaf remaining in the glorious red-and-gold fili-gree-pattern wallpaper that hadn't faded much at all. Two immense mahogany sofas upholstered in burgundy velvet sat to either side of the hall, furniture too heavy to move and so stiffly uncomfortable that no one ever sat on them for long.

The four men receiving the visitors didn't go near the sofas. All in suits of varying shades of dark gray, and all of a certain age, for this angle clearly revealed one grizzled pate and three with thinning hair. Augusta's father was there, along with George, thirdly the Black man on retainer as the Institute's primary lawyer, and lastly the oldest White man whom Augusta only recognized as the State undersecretary for magic after he turned to say something to George.

Six people faced them: four men and two women. The quillwork on their clothing marked them as Haudenosaunee. It was harder to catch their features in the distance and angled light, especially as the men didn't remove their feathered hats nor the women their heavily beaded caps, but one of the men and the women appeared to be elders. The younger men might include the Kanien'ke-há:ka who'd driven the autowagon down to the Institute earlier and gone away without answer.

The aged man stepped forward and said something in a liquid language. Kanien'kéha, no doubt. Although Augusta didn't understand it, her father had insisted that Danny, at least, take lessons in it after the Reconstituted Congress's recent law mandating state schools teach local Indigenous languages alongside European. Danny had taken to it as a duck to water, wandering the house repeating words and phrases without ever explaining any of them.

Their father showed no reaction, but the other three made up even though as far as Augusta knew none of them spoke Kanien'kéha. George drew himself up, seeming to gain several millimeters. The lawyer pursed his mouth, fingers steepled before his chest. The undersecretary nodded.

The visitor continued, shifting to unaccented English with barely a pause. "The royá:ner asked us to come discuss with you the matter of the place you call Sanctuary Hall."

"Please come in and let us speak in comfort." Augusta's father waved at the front office, which had once been the parlor.

The oldest man, a younger man, and the women nodded and entered, followed by the Institute representatives. Two men remained in the hall. One walked over to inspect a sofa and said something soft and low to his fellow.

The other turned around slowly, studying the walls, then looked up. A familiar light-brown face smiled and waved at Augusta and the other watchers.

Floorboards squeaked across the way as the others went back to their business. Jake was the last. He paused to glance over at Augusta and jerk his chin at her office in a clear message. She stuck her chin back out at him but returned to her usual duties.

Concentrating on the task before her proved difficult. It wasn't much, merely lists of the various people who'd stayed at the Institute over the last year for inclusion in the annual report to the State. The binders mostly stayed for a few weeks and then went home, often more set in their ways. The pathwalkers came and went, sometimes returning several times. The speakers with minor gifts rarely remained long. Those with powerful gifts eventually went to Sanctuary Hall, where regular visitations by winds and rains were less of an issue—though they rarely lasted long regardless.

The last made for depressing reading, given the number marked either as deceased or missing and presumed deceased.

Had her brother and sister and cousin ever appeared on similar lists to another state? Her siblings surely not, at least not yet. Even as powerful as they'd seemed to grow, they would still be in their late teens and very early twenties. Nanette, on the other hand, would be in her late twenties, and she'd already dwindled to saying almost nothing seven years earlier.

The floors creaked, and distant vibrations rippled

through to tingle Augusta's toes. Nothing new. This was an old house, and rarely silent. Still, after a few moments the regularity of the creaks and squeaks broke Augusta's concentration.

Louder, closer, as someone walked up the stairs and around the doorway to her office. She sat back in her chair, cushions shifting beneath her.

One of the younger guests stood there, hat in long-fingered hands that stroked the feathers lining the curved sides. Short black hair slick with sweat lined his head. He was about her age or maybe a little older, given the weathered edge to his face. A hint of pine hung about him. He nodded. "Greetings, unbinder."

"Greetings." Augusta tidied the piles on her desk, nearly sending a few papers floating off before she grabbed them and pressed them onto a pile. "How can I help you?"

"They call me . . ." He followed the English words with a long string of liquid syllables.

"Ah." She swallowed, sure that she'd have to hear his name pronounced a half-dozen times to have even a hope of saying it properly.

His lips twisted, and he tilted his head to the side. "I am also called Summer."

For a brief moment, a wide smile as warm as summer flashed across his face, then it was gone.

"Augusta Deyo." She laid a hand on her chest. Much as she wanted to stop there, she couldn't resist asking. "Why did you call me unbinder?"

"Is it not true?" He glanced at the empty chair on the other side of the desk and lifted an eyebrow.

She nodded. "Yes, but . . ."

"I saw how you looked at the binding on the water

spirit powering our wagon earlier." The chair legs scraped against the floor, but the seat held when he sat down. "Surely only someone who can bind and unbind might gaze with such care on what keeps the spirit there. It's a properly made agreement, offering benefit to either side."

"Yes, yes I saw that. You guessed from just that one . . ." She wouldn't have guessed—then again, she never had to. Most of the binders she met were fellow research subjects at the Institute, because she rarely went to the capital or city hall or even the post offices where local binders and freelancers passing through put up notices of their avail- ability, and people wanting bindings done did likewise. So much of her life was her family and the Institute.

"Your father is known as an expert on unbinding, for all that his gift is small. I've heard he taught you"—Summer waved at her—"much of what he knows, and that your power far exceeds his."

"I'm not that powerful. Only mid-range."

"It is not your power that brings me here, but your knowledge. Would you consider a trade of favors?" He offered his hand. "A one-time exchange."

Was Summer a binder? She couldn't tell, only guess because he was here talking about bindings.

"No?" Again an eyebrow lifted.

"I can't guarantee I can answer your questions." She sat back, resting her hands flat on the desk. "Or you mine."

"Fair enough."

Feverish warmth filled her cheeks. Try. Try what? For seven years she'd tried to hold her family together, what was left of it.

He offered information? Fine, why not ask what she most wanted to know—or what he might know about that. "Seven years ago, my mother and two siblings and cousin left and have not been heard from since. Can you help me find them?"

His turn to sit back, surprise on his face. Whatever had he thought she'd ask? He had to know something of the Deyo family, if he knew her father trained her in unbinding, and who would learn that without also hearing about the disappearance of half of her family?

Her lungs ached from holding her breath, muscles quivering as she stayed still in hopes—but not expectations.

"I know of no finders among the Haudenosaunee who would be able to assist you." Summer shook his head.

"Of course not." Pathwalkers were rare enough there was no guarantee any lived among the Haudenosaunee. Augusta's belly ached—she'd asked a pathwalker visiting the Institute a similar question once and received such a look in return. Not to mention the sizable fee the pathwalker required to even consider looking, because they specialized in finding places not people.

"I cannot give you what you desire, but if you will answer my question, I will owe you an equal answer."

"Go ahead." Her father hadn't taught her secrets, merely worked with her through book after book about bindings, how to place them, and how to undo them, then let her practice with regularity.

"There is a place that has been bound for centuries. Bound and rebound, with layers of bindings atop one another." He leaned forward. "The winds howl at the borders. Storms rush there but go around the place, never over. The place gets gentle rain. Lightning cracks the skies without ever touching any part of that land."

A place long-bound . . . given the other Kanien'kehá:ka downstairs meeting with her father, Augusta found it impossible not to wonder if this was connected, but she kept her lips pressed shut rather than interrupt.

"We have offered ease. Layer by layer, we have sought to undo the bindings and free the lands to be as they would and restore the weather to its usual patterns." Gazing straight at her, he stretched out his hands to either side. "Yet nothing has changed."

An interesting puzzle, but . . . she frowned. "Your question?"

"How can the land remain bound despite all our labor to undo the bindings? The very earth remakes the bindings even as we seek to free it."

Augusta studied him, seeking any indication why he was asking her. Surely he was a binder and had participated in the efforts to undo the bindings—in which case he was far more experienced than she in dealing with plots of land. She'd mostly bound or unbound small ties—bushes and trees and minor waterways, which were easy enough to reduce to nothing.

All of which left the suspicion that it was a trick question. That he had the answer, just wanted to know if she knew it too. Which she didn't, never having visited Sanctuary Hall—assuming that was where he meant—to see the layers of bindings and the earth that evidently didn't want to be free.

His fingers twitched, hands still outstretched.

"Give me a moment to think." Augusta crossed her arms over her chest.

Summer pulled back but drummed his fingers against the desk in an odd rhythm or melody that kept switching so that she couldn't predict where it would go.

"Perhaps there's a knot, a condition unmet." She shrugged, but the matter nagged at her and required more serious consideration. "Or the binding is at a deeper level that holds the surface ones in place even when they appear to be banished. Or there are multiple bindings that have tangled over time, and you must find the key to each separately."

"Or deal with them all at once, but we have undone all that we can see." He grimaced, but stopped tapping the desk in favor of stroking his hat.

"Then find someone who can see differently, or . . ." In any binding, details made a difference. Why keep up the pretense of it being somewhere unspecified? "This land, is it Sanctuary Hall?"

Summer nodded.

"I don't know much about the Hall, but the first part was built back in the 1600s."

"By your ancestors." He waved at her. "The tales of my people say they were fleeing something."

"They left England in a hurry,"—there was something more to it, but Augusta couldn't remember it at the moment—"and purchased the land from your people."

Summer shook his head, nose wrinkling. "They took."

"Oh." Augusta bit her lips. The earth didn't care about ownership, or so Augusta had always been told. The deeper the earth, the longer it thought, in centuries and millennia, and the less it cared for shorter terms. Yet if the Whistles who built the Hall thought they'd purchased the land, that would have been part of their binding.

If they'd even made a binding.

"*Did* they make a binding with the land back then?" Augusta tucked her hair behind her ears, even though it hadn't fallen forward. "Magic was weak and most people didn't even know why worked stone and metal were so important in settling crops and raising buildings."

"*Your* people may not have known."

"Yes, but . . ." Augusta frowned. "Then who made the binding?"

"Someone of your people." Summer shrugged. "It was one reason my ancestors agreed to let them stay on the land. Our histories of that time say that binding lay so heavy on the earth it repudiated all attempts to undo it."

"Which means whatever is resisting being unbound is ancient. Centuries old, at the least. And if it was done by one of my ancestors, from Europe, who didn't know much about magic, they'd have made it heavy and thick, with iron instead of steel." She rubbed her hands together. The agreement between them pushed her to do more, a weight on her stomach. He had deferred his part until later, but all the same an urgency beat in her blood to be of assistance. "Didn't the earliest bindings require some kind of exchange? Documents or . . . or wampum?"

"No, we did not use wampum for currency." His lips tightened, but his gaze turned inward. "This binding was not between my ancestors and yours, but yours and the earth."

"By all the stories I know of my ancestors, bargains with land involved something physical—a sword or stone or . . . Maybe there's a representation, or more than one, that must be destroyed or undone to remove the last bindings."

"Something physical, yes, that could be. If we can only find it." Shaking his head, he rose and gave her a half-bow. "Thank you."

"You owe me." Augusta pushed back her chair and stood straight, hands on her desk. "A fair exchange."

"I have cause now to seek out a finder and will ask them if they are willing to offer any assistance, though they may only tell you which way to go. If not, you may ask of me equal information. Leave word at the Kanien'kehá:ka offices in the state house, and it will reach me."

With barely a creak, he was gone, leaving the unfilled binding hanging in the air between them—and an extra reason for Augusta to retrace her mother's steps and see Sanctuary Hall.

CHAPTER 5

QUESTIONS, ANSWERS, AND QUESTIONS

Augusta expected her interest in going to Sanctuary Hall to fade that evening, in the comfort of home. Not so. Home had changed. Only four chairs surrounded the dining room table. The others had vanished, to the attic or wherever her father wanted—because who else would have gone behind Augusta's back to ask the staff to move them?

For the first time, Augusta sat at the foot of the table, in her mother's place and yet not her mother's place, for she sat on the chair her mother had decorated with cardinals for Augusta not the osprey she'd kept for herself. Dressed in the same clothes Augusta had worn all day, now a bit wrinkled but still good—and similar to what Mother had usually worn. Augusta had talked with their housekeeper and planned the meals, but if asked afterward what she'd eaten she wouldn't have been able to describe a thing. Each bite tasted of nothing at best, ashes at worst.

She didn't belong here, not in this place at the table—not in this room with so much more space and so few chairs. What next—would Father have it painted a different color? Hang new art on the walls? Marry and install a new wife where Augusta now sat, sending her back to the side while someone else chose the menus and ran the house?

Worse, every time Augusta closed her eyes, memories of her mother passed through. Her mother in this very chair, at dinner. Pale of face, with signs she'd been weeping, but her mouth curved in a big smile that didn't reach her eyes. Mother's voice rang out in Augusta's head promising to stay.

She'd vanished the next day.

Augusta pushed her food around on the plate, blobs of white and brown and green, and didn't talk much. No one did. Father was grumpy at his end, cutting his roast chicken into ever smaller bites and gnashing his teeth against the fork several times. Jake stared off into the distance, hardly looking at his plate although he managed to eat all his chicken and potatoes and carrots without disturbing a single pea. Danny cleaned his plate twice; maybe he was on the verge of a growth spurt. Augusta would have to check the trunks in the attic for Jake's old clothes to see if any were still suitable for wear.

Or not. That was what Mother would have done if she were here.

How much of Augusta's life involved doing what Mother would have done? Even her interest in going to the Hall, because Mother had been there. Still, perhaps in tracing her mother's departure backward, Augusta would find a way forward.

Jake vanished after dinner, off and out of the house gone who-knew-where. Danny retreated to his room—to study, or so one could hope.

Before Augusta might do the same, her father invited her into the study to talk.

Or listen.

How long since she had last ventured in? Long enough that the room surprised her. It was very much Father's, with few touches of Mother. The books had belonged to both, but most of the easily readable titles gilded on the leather spines spoke of Father's interests, not mothers. A faint haze of tobacco clung to the two big, brown leather chairs, matching cushioned footrests, and the slightly scarred side tables next to them. Even the bright red-and-blue rug, with signs of wear and a few ash-stains.

A flicker of gold caught the lamplight as Augusta settled onto the chair that didn't have a Father-sized impression in the cushions. Her father eased into his seat, fiddling with his pipe. Familiar actions: tamping down the tobacco, lighting, and taking that first all-important puff. His hands cradled the wooden curved pipe as usual—but gold glinted on the wrong hand.

He'd moved his wedding ring.

The smoke should be comforting. It had been in the for days, weeks, months after Mother had left, when Augusta so often woke screaming in the night and Father was the one who came to comfort her.

But just now, with her stomach full of whatever it was she'd eaten, the smoke made her cough and press a hand against her belly in hopes she didn't bring it back up.

All the while, she stared at the ring which looked the same and yet completely different on her father's other hand. "It's really happening."

"The lawyer will have the papers ready to file next week." Her father nodded and puffed away, running a hand through hair she hadn't realized was thinning quite so much until she'd gotten a good look at the bald spot at the center from above. More change. "It won't be quick. May take a half-year, but it will go through."

"What if she comes back?" Augusta wove her hands together, wrists hard against her midsection.

Her father froze. Blinked, with the possible glint of tears although his cheeks remained dry. "She won't. Not unless . . . she won't."

"Not unless what?"

He puffed away, for a minute. Two. Three, before he finally asked, "Don't you know?"

"No! I don't . . . one day she was here, and then she was gone." Augusta gritted her teeth and eased back. Propped her feet on the footrest, plum skirt-pants dark against the buttery leather. "Jake says she asked him to go with her, and he wouldn't, but why didn't she ask me?"

"She did."

"What?" Augusta jerked back upright, feet flat on the carpet.

"You truly don't remember. . ."

"Would I ask you if I did?"

Father knocked ashes into a tray, turned away from Augusta, but his words came through clear enough. "She asked you to go. You wanted her to stay."

Mother had asked Augusta. She closed her eyes and willed something, anything, to come back. Mother appeared in memory's eyes, pale and fierce and holding Augusta's hands so tight her fingers hurt for hours after. It was several days before her departure, maybe a week or two. They'd been in the parlor, Augusta still in her school uniform of blue and white tunic over skirt-pants while Mother was in disarray, hair half-down her back and dust staining her creamy blouse and beige skirt-pants, and mud clinging to her boots.

Mother saying there must be some other solution. She wouldn't have her children confined and locked up away from the world. If Father and the Institute couldn't find a solution here, then mother would go on her own search. The speaker power ran in her side of the family, and she couldn't let her babies suffer for something they got from her. She didn't have enough power here to protect them, but there had to be somewhere they'd be safe.

What had Augusta done? Pled for Mother to slow down, to take time and stay and talk to Father. He'd help keep Frank and Callie safe and sane. Mother had to stay, she belonged here.

Then the memory blurred. They were up in her parents' room, with suitcases laid out on the bed. Mother holding Augusta's hands, eyes wide, as she promised to not to leave.

"She said she would stay." Augusta knew that much, even if she still couldn't recall Mother asking *her* to go.

"She couldn't." Father set his pipe in the ash tray and leaned forward. "Your mother loves you, never doubt that. I'm sure she still loves me as well." More tears dampening the corners of his eyes, this time trickling out, in mute testimony that he returned her love. "But your brother and sister and cousin needed her."

"They could have stayed."

"Frank and Callie were powerful speakers, air and water though thank God no touch of fire. Young as they were, they had started to talk to us and their friends less and listen to the elements more, Callie favoring air and Frank water. If they were still here—we haven't found a cure, a way to keep speakers from being lost to spirits." Father braced his head in his hands. "And then there was your cousin.

Nanette hadn't said more than a word to anyone in weeks. Water spirits kept visiting her here, rains and trickles to the point the neighbors complained and the State was on the verge of taking her into custody and ordering her sent to Sanctuary Hall. Your mother worried about what would happen to them, night after night and day after day, until I yelled at her stop. We'd do everything within our power, I told her, but we couldn't protect them from themselves."

His shoulders jerked, a thick shiver rippling through him. When he lifted his head, his face was wet and eyes haunted.

"She decided she had to leave and take them away. It was then or never. She even asked me to join her, although I think she half hated me by then, but I would not leave the Institute, which I considered then and now one of the best chances to find a solution." He sighed. "I hoped she'd find a cure somewhere, since I haven't, but then she'd have come back or written or something. The years just kept rolling by with no word."

It made sense, but also it didn't because of that memory of Augusta holding her mother's hands, or was that the other way around? And mother agreeing to stay.

"She loved . . . loves you, loves us, but they needed her and her protection more. And she always did need to be needed, to protect." Father cupped Augusta's cheeks. "The last thing she asked of me, before she left, was to protect you."

Augusta leaned into the caress, then pulled away and walked to the nearest bookshelf. Ran a finger across the smooth spines of volumes of scientific and philosophical treatises on magic.

Behind her, the scratch of a match and burst of sulfur indicated her father had relit his pipe.

"Visiting Sanctuary Hall made her decide to leave," Augusta said. Mother had gone the day after her visit.

"She'd been thinking of it anyway, but . . . yes." Father nodded. "That was the final straw."

"George invited me, and I might go there." Augusta settled back onto the chair. She toed off her shoes and pulled her legs up under her, the better to warm her feet.

"Maybe it would help, but . . ." Father shook his head and sighed.

"What?"

"You won't see what she saw. It's changed since then." Father glanced around his study and chuckled. "Changed far more than this. Seven years ago, George was still in the early stages of fixing it back up. He'd only managed to buy it back, with the Institute's help, a few years earlier."

"Bought it?" Augusta asked. "Didn't it always belong in the family?"

"Close, but not quite. My uncle Trey—"

"George Whistle the Third."

Father gaze grew distant and he let loose a smoky huff. "A nice man."

She had few recollections of her great-uncle. "He used to give Jake and me and the other cousins lollypops whenever he saw us."

"That's about as much attention he gave his own children, too, a lollypop when he saw them, then a pat on the head and he sent them off to stay with relatives while he and my aunt enjoyed a sparkling social life." Another huff from Father. "But he wasn't any good with money. Or rather he was good at spending and making bets on stocks that failed. He nearly went bankrupt several times and pulled himself back out, but in the end nothing could save him. That was when I arranged to buy the house here in town, for the Institute, and keep a suite for him to live in, your aunt having passed away a few years earlier."

"The rooms Mrs. O'Leary has now." Augusta might have been taken to visit him a time or three.

"George and his wife moved in with her family, in their house in town, though he complained constantly about the crowding." Father took a deep breath and let out a smoky O.

Mute commentary on George's complaint. Augusta had seen that house—it was a mansion easily twice the size of the Institute and three times as ornate.

"Trey's brother and sisters and children, except for George, scattered from Boston to Baltimore," Father continued. "But Uncle Trey kept spending, and by the end he lost everything. George got to Sanctuary Hall just in time to buy it back from the bailiffs—but not before most of the furnishings and fixtures were sold. It was in lousy condition because Trey hadn't kept it up, but George loved it and he's spent the last decade bringing it back to what the house he remembers as a child, when our grandparents were still alive and had family gatherings every summer and winter." Father laughed, gaze going distant and lips curving in a soft smile. "We used try and stay up at night to catch sight of the ghost."

Father's remembered pleasure warmed Augusta. She'd get to see a place he had fond memories of. "It's haunted?"

"Supposedly."

"Mrs. O'Leary's talked about ghosts, but I've never seen any."

"There aren't any around here, but farther out from the city . . . yes." He puffed on his pipe. "Fortunately for us, at least, the ghosts in this area are voluntary, at least so far as I've heard."

"Voluntary?" Augusta ran a hand through her hair, tucking curls behind her ears. Binders, pathwalkers, and speakers she knew, but it sometimes seemed every time she turned around, especially today, she learned of some new complication. It made her long for the comfort of predictability, of the formerly unchanging house and regular routines.

"Not bound."

It took her a moment to work through the implications —and the horror. It was common knowledge that binders' powers worked on humans as well as the elements. How else could they create balanced agreements between lands, waters, winds, and humans? But Augusta had always assumed the appearance of bound ghosts in gothic novels to be fiction. "People bind spirits to remain after death?"

"People bind all manner of things, wittingly and unwittingly, as we know all too well." Her father sighed. "Supposedly the ghost is Martha Montgomery Whistle, our many times great-grandmother. She's buried in a crypt on the property. She was the one who named the place Sanctuary Hall, for that matter, or so the tale goes." Father twiddled his fingers around the stem of his pipe. "She was the wife of the regicide Whistle who signed the death warrant for Charles I of England, and they fled when Charles II took the throne—convinced that the king would send soldiers or assassins after the whole family, although of course we know now he didn't.

"They ran all the way across the ocean, taking the whole family with them, and kept running once they arrived in the New World until they reached the vale and great-however-many-greats grandfather negotiated with the Haudenosaunee to acquire the land. He was a binder, or she was, or both—binding runs in the family. That's where you and I get it."

The bits and pieces Augusta remembered fit together into a coherent whole, except for the ghost part. Ghosts existing was one thing, having one in the family quite another. "And now the Haudenosaunee want it back."

"Because of extreme weather, which happens when you have a lot of disconnected speakers in close proximity." Father shook his head. "George will never give it up as long as he has breath. He even made arrangements to get money from the State for housing those speakers, though he had to turn the title over to the Institute to handle the legalities. He'll do anything so long as he can keep restoring the Hall, which shows how much he loves it, even spend time and money caring for speakers in their last years. Yes," he said, gaze fixing on Augusta, "yes, I think going there might be a fine thing. You'll understand why your mother took the others and fled—or you won't."

"Would you want Frank and Callie there?"

"I haven't visited in years, not since your mother . . ." He settled back in his chair, shoulders hunching. "It's George's business, just as the Institute is mine."

"Though that doesn't stop George from sticking his nose in the Institute." Augusta frowned, studying her father who was back fiddling with his pipe.

"It's just him considering himself the head of the Whistle family." Father laid aside his pipe long enough to catch her eye. "You go there, just . . . promise to come back here before you do anything else?"

"Where do you think I'd go?" Augusta didn't meet his gaze. She didn't know where else, but there might be somewhere, and wondered what he thought.

"It's not what I think that matters, if it's *you* going." He grabbed her hand and pressed it. "What matters more is, I want to know you're all right."

Just so had Mother held Augusta after her visit. Or was that how Augusta had held onto her? She laid her hand atop, sandwiching his. "I promise."

CHAPTER 6

OUT OF THE CITY

Augusta hadn't realized she'd be traveling the old-fashioned way: by horse and carriage, and in the backward-facing seat of the carriage at that. The horses smelled, quite apart from how often they let loose with a stream of manure that the wagon wheels frequently rolled through. Did the drivers not even try to avoid it? Horses walked no faster than Augusta could have if she'd gotten out and moved her own legs—certainly slower than wind or water-powered autowagons. True, the road through the woody hills was unpaved and mostly a matter of parallel ruts in the hard earth, save for places where the ruts doubled to allow opposing traffic to pass, but still.

For the fifteenth time in the hour, she stretched and, as discreetly as possible, tried to loosen her thin yellow linen blouse from sticking to her back and front. Her jacket she'd stripped off earlier and put aside. No doubt the soft blue fabric was getting hopelessly wrinkled, stuffed between her and the side of the carriage. There was little air circulation around her legs, and her skirt-pants stuck to her legs in patches. Inside her shoes, her toes sweated and itched. She ran her fingers through her short bob, trying to keep the strands from plastering to her head and neck. The sun and motion kept away insects, at least.

No one else seemed to suffer quite so much, or they managed to hide it. Cousins Susanna and Marianna, George's wife and older daughter, couldn't be as cool and collected as they seemed. Surely they were sweltering in their fine pale-blue three-piece dress-suits, plus blouses and shoes and long blond hair swept into updos that left their pale necks bare. Yet they ignored the thin streaks of perspiration along the sides of their faces.

George and his younger daughter both rode horses rather than squeeze into the carriage—which was quite full enough with three people, so Augusta silently thanked them for that—and while they had broad hats to keep off the sun, they seemed otherwise quite content. At least, his younger daughter did, mostly keeping near the carriage and chatting with her brother George Whistle V, better known as Quint, atop with the driver. George kept busy roaming up and down the caravan of wagons and carriages carting enough supplies to surely last a year rather than a summer.

So many people! Wagon drivers, grooms, maids, and who-knew-what-all else. Augusta hadn't ever seen half so many on her occasional visits to Susanna's family's mansion in town. Father employed a housekeeper and a maid-of-all-work at the house, in addition to the staff at the Institute, and Augusta had always thought that quite luxurious. Then again, her hands had ink stains while Susanna and Marianna had no marks on their fingers or so Augusta guessed, since both wore gloves. Gloves on a hot summer day? Perhaps the thin cambric didn't stick to their palms, but Augusta preferred to be glove-free.

The carriage led the procession, which should have left them clear of the dust kicked up by hooves and wheels. Instead, at best Augusta caught glimpses of hills and trees amid a fair amount of dust. Two vehicles behind the carriage rode the air and earth speaker from the Institute. He might no longer be able to communicate in words, but breezes loved him and kept his wagon free of dust at the expense of others, including the carriage.

Dust and sweat and a bumpy road. What joy. Why they couldn't take autowagons she still didn't understand. She'd muttered something to that effect early in the trip and gotten a level look from Susanna.

"This is how my husband's family always traveled to the Hall. It's tradition."

And that was that. Despite the hint of resignation in Susanna's voice, the firm pronouncement clearly put Augusta in her place as the poor cousin who didn't under-stand—not a way Augusta had seen herself before.

Then a moment later, the older woman turned to her daughter and started right back into the serious business of planning the whole of the summer—who was visiting when, which rooms to assign them, what games and activi-ties to prepare for, and what could be done indoors if the weather didn't cooperate.

All of which confused Augusta. How big was the Hall if the family planned house party after house party while also hosting at least a half-dozen disconnected speakers and the staff needed to care for them?

Just another indication of her status as the poor cousin, no doubt.

With their chatter filling the carriage, Augusta leaned against the side and stared out the narrow window. Despite the ebb and flow of dust, beautiful scene after scene passed by: lush valleys filled with greenery; woods mixed with fields and glades; and hills blending into mountains.

Few humans, and those mostly in the fields at work—save for figures standing atop hills or rises and watching the procession move through. This was Kanien'kehá:ka territory even if the road belonged to the State. In the span of an hour, she picked out five watchers.

The sight irritated George when he took a break in the carriage, warming the small enclosure further as he panted and drained a bottle of water. Heat and sweat poured off him from his half of the seat next to Augusta. "Safe passage guaranteed on the roads, hah. I should bring them up for harassment."

"Whatever you wish, dear." Susanna nodded, hands busy copying room assignments into a notebook from scratch paper. Her mechanical pencil scratched, but it explained the lack of ink stains.

"Oh, Father." Marianna covered her mouth, eyes wide, then tilted her head to one side. "Can you do that? Who would you bring them up before?"

"All the way to Congress, if I must." George glared at Marianna, who ducked her head. "The Hall is mine, and they know it." He sighed, shoulders slumping. "How can I give it up after so many generations? It's where we belong." Turning to the side, he nudged Augusta. "You'll see. You're a Whistle too, as are your father and brothers, no matter that you call yourselves Deyos."

"I look forward to seeing it," Augusta said.

"This is the first year we can really entertain. The work on the house and outbuildings is mostly done. Though, this isn't the best time to visit, or the best way." George leaned back against the carriage wall, his outstretched legs forcing his wife and daughter to squeeze back against their seat.

His gaze went distant, face soft. "When I was little, we always went up to the Hall for Christmas. Sometimes the lake would freeze in time, so we could take a sledge across the ice for the last leg. So cold your breath froze, even tucked in layers of furs. Bells ringing, sweet on the ears, letting Grandpapa and Grandmama know we were on our way. The house glowing against the hillside with candles set in every window. We'll do that this winter, as soon as the lake freezes."

Susanna and Marianna continued a soft conversation on the far side, casting smiles and nods at George as he rolled off story after story of Christmases and summer holidays spent at the Hall. Of his grandparents fussing over him, and making the whole of the house his treasure.

Lovely as the stories were, they all ended the same way: determination to recreate the glorious home he remembered.

He only stopped recounting memories when the caravan paused at a village near the southern end of a long, thin lake.

Augusta managed to remember her manners and wait for the others to leave the carriage, only to hiss as she stepped out. Her legs cramped from so long in a small space. Much as she wanted the rest and refreshments promised at the inn—an overgrown compilation of several large white houses—she waved off her relations, saying she needed to walk first.

Pushing past the first bursts of pain, she tottered down a gravel-and-grass lane toward the lake. The village was a mix of styles, with a large inn and several other tall buildings at the center surrounded by one-story cottages, taller houses, and several camping sites half-filled with tents ranging from pristine to grimy. A single log cabin was set slightly higher and to the side with a view of the lake. Water birds called overhead, ducking and rising as they dealt with the breezes still circling the wagon carrying the speaker.

The citizens going about their business spoke in a mixture of languages—English, French, Dutch, and above all Kanien'kéha. The village was situated within Kanien'ke- há:ka land, one of the places they allowed people who wanted to live in their territory to stay for a while and prove themselves, and their elders were much in evidence.

A dozen different cooking smells—peppers, beef, chicken, and something musty-spicy—combined to reduce her interest in lunch though she regretted not having stopped for a drink.

Clouds skittered in the sky, all fluffy and white turning into blurry reflections in the gentle waves below. Across the narrow the lake lay a verdant swathe of green grass angling up from a narrow beach to a plateau. Few trees grew there, though many tall leafy spans rose from the hill behind.

The Hall rose three stories high at the center rectangle, two stories for the lengthy wings to either side. The dark-gray stones must have come from a nearby quarry, as they fit the surroundings and matched a stony hillside farther down the lake shore. Though surely created in fits and starts, the various parts melded together into a harmonic whole. Several ruddy brick chimneys and broad swathes of roof tiles topped the man-made cliff that was the Hall. Those within might consider themselves in control of all they could survey. So many windows glinting in the sunlight, it was easy to imagine the warm golden glow of candles on a dark winter night. A gravel drive circled around the front, the far end emerging from a deep wealth of trees, but the Hall faced the lake, not the woods.

Additional buildings were arrayed behind the main edifice, most stone as well but one with white sides. Down below, closer to the shore yet well above the beach, the front of a stone edifice sat flush against the slope with a double door that glinted dark metal in the sunlight. Thick vegetation surrounded it save where a thin trail curved away from the grassy lawn to lead to the doors. An ice house, perhaps, or a crypt.

Everything glowed with light and health. The greens of lawn and trees were greener, the buildings solid and deep-rooted, and the woods seemed to curve protectively around the house. The waters of the lake lapped against the beach, sometimes encroaching high but always retreating. No matter how hard the growing winds blew over the lake, only the very tips of the trees swayed.

Her mother had come home from visiting this and fled?

Footsteps crunched on the gravel, then George appeared at her side. He carried two bottles, both beaded with moisture, and offered her one.

The cool glass nearly slipped through her fingers until she got a better grip. Unscrewing the top, she sipped at the lemon-infused water rather than cool her throat too quickly.

"That's where we're going. Not too far, now, and we'll be home." Such satisfaction in that one word.

Augusta hesitated, then asked, "isn't it technically owned by the Institute?"

"Not much longer now. I've been working all hours to bring it back to what it was." George rubbed his bottle against his forehead. "Maybe you can help me."

"Do what?" Augusta swallowed a cool draft, shivering as it went down. Or was that due to a breeze whipping up into a wind and pushing the clouds across the lake? "I mean, I want to see it all, everything you've done and what you're making it into."

"I'll give you the full tour, top to bottom and side to side." George gripped her shoulder and gave a firm squeeze. "Then you'll understand."

"I look forward to it."

The wind whipped up a storm out of nowhere over the lake. Waves lashed, topped with white froth. Lightning flashed in the sky, although it didn't hit the ground. Instead, the bolts whirled in circles.

Nevertheless, a hint of fire and ash doubled back over the lake to fall on the village. A flake landed in Augusta's uncapped bottle—or so she guessed. For she still tasted ash an hour later when the convoy reached the bridge over the river and the final approach to the Hall.

CHAPTER 7

TOURING SANCTUARY HALL

"And this is the servants' stairway," George proclaimed as he led Augusta along the upper hall.

Made of gorgeous and rare tiger maple, the staircase deserved admiration. It lacked curlicues or adornments and needed neither. The plain lines suited the wood, which gleamed from recent polishing. The pine scent lingered in the air to the point Augusta tasted it. Despite the cool morning air, it was warm to the touch thanks to rays of light angling in through tall windows in the bright yellow walls.

"Lovely." How many times had she said that or similar words? Truly, the house was beautifully designed and constructed from the public rooms to the servants' quarters, despite having grown over the years or decades, but she was getting a bit tired of admiring things. She'd dressed for comfort in fabric suitable for the cool of morning and the warmth of afternoon, from her tunic down to her soft-soled leather shoes. All the same, her feet hurt from traipsing about uttering the requisite oohs and aahs.

George hadn't seemed so energetic when she'd greeted him at the breakfast table, both he and she having risen far earlier than anyone else in the family. He'd pulled on a blue sweater over a white shirt and light-blue pants, but his face was so drawn she couldn't tell where shirt stopped and neck started. Coffee had revived him, and he'd happily led her on a wandering path through every public and guest room, down hallways galore, and among the servants' working and sleeping quarters top-to-bottom.

Augusta stroked the smooth railing, steps barely creaking as they descended. The lower end of the stair ended near a corner where two servant halls met. Soft yellow paint covered the walls, the trim in white setting off doorways and the big multi-paned windows looking out onto a courtyard. Gray stones formed the courtyard flooring, a stark contrast to the gleaming wood floors indoors. Two grates in the courtyard led to underground cisterns that collected rainwater for use in washing and watering the garden.

The sizzle of onions and peppers floated through the air, although Augusta had lost track and wasn't sure if the cooks prepared breakfast for the rest of the family or had started on lunch.

The mostly overcast sky didn't help her figure out the time. Faint sunbeams made it through the cloud cover but seemed to come from a half-dozen angles.

On the ground floor, George led her down a branching corridor. As they passed a room filled with china to serve dozens, the window offered a view of the hillside behind the house. Augusta stepped in, lured by the soft breeze slipping in through a gap where someone had left the window ajar. Far enough away from the cooking smells, the light gust carried a sweeter, more natural pine scent mixed with roses and lilacs. In the distance, the wind blew strong enough to make the tree tops bend—but not closer in as though harsh winds couldn't come too near the house.

"My sisters and I used to play hide-and-seek when we visited our grandparents. We might go anywhere in the house, as long as we didn't make trouble for the servants." George herded Augusta out of the room and further down the hall, pointing out places he'd hid once upon a time. "Grandfather played too. He'd pretend he was a bear when he found one of us, and roar,"—he paused long enough to stretch to his full height, fingers curved as claws—"and we'd run, and run—up or down, any which way, trying to find Grandmother, who was our safe haven."

"That must've been fun."

"Glorious." George brushed a hand along the wall, gaze distant and steps slowing. "At Christmas, every inch was decorated. Pine boughs woven through the railings. I've told the servants to only use pine polish. That's what this should smell like all the time."

"Lovely." Another repetition. Augusta needed to find another word or two to use.

He jumped from story to story, each and every one featuring his grandparents and siblings with nary a reference to his father or mother.

"I know, I'm an old fogy living in the past. My daughters tell me so regularly." Fondness and humor layered his voice, gaze remaining distant. "I might've said the same to my grandfather when I was young. I didn't understand then."

He stopped, leaning against the wall. Augusta tucked herself in behind him to leave the hall free as a footman in a royal-blue uniform pushed a cart laden with covered dishes to the public rooms. The scent of eggs and onions and peppers lingered behind.

"It's a wonderful place. So different from the mansion where the Institute is," Augusta said. The uniforms alone made for a notable difference. All of the livery was royal blue with touches of silver. Even the maids wore blue dresses with frilly white aprons over, in contrast to the pale blue of the Institute—which was also a lot easier to wash. Augusta hadn't managed to figure out just how large the house was, but it seemed to have a lot more servants than the Institute, where Mrs. O'Leary regularly corralled scientists to help move items around.

"The difference was night and day." George started up again, stroking the yellow wall. "My father's taste for gilt and my mother's for ornamentation won out in the city, even before my grandparents passed away. *They* always preferred the simplicity of the country, as do I."

Simplicity was not a word that Augusta would choose to describe the Hall. It had too many rooms, halls, servants. Still, it was less gilded, with plain furniture and materials of the best quality, making it more comfortable in many ways.

Rather nice as a place to get away, though she wouldn't want to stay long. Too big and rambling, even more of a contrast to her family's home in the city. Being here was comfy, but already part of her wanted to go home where she knew where everything was and could walk from bedroom to dining room blindfolded.

Her desire to leave was odd considering the wonderful, warm, family atmosphere of the night before. George, Susanna, and their children drew Augusta to join them in all manner of games with ample teasing and jokes to keep everything merry. George beamed all evening long, telling his children until they rolled their eyes how much this brought back memories of playing the same card games with his siblings and grandparents, and how he hoped the house would always be in the family, a place for this kind of gathering.

His son had promised. His younger daughter pouted briefly over the clear assumption her brother would get the house, but ceased when her father sent a sharp look her way. Her brother reminded her she'd always be welcome.

Had Augusta and Jake and Danny played any games since their mother and other siblings left? She dug up vague memories of evenings of cards or colorful boards spilled across the living room floor, but they'd been quieter, more subdued than before—and never in the dining room, with the empty chairs a constant reminder.

George paused at the end of a cool hall edging another courtyard, one side bearing doors leading into pantries and storage rooms. The very far end had a stone floor and wide double door that surely led to the outside, while on the right was another hall heading back toward the main part of the house.

At which Augusta realized she hadn't seen or heard or anything else—breezes, indoor rain—of the speakers.

"Hmm." George gave her sharp look, much the same as he'd aimed at his daughter the night before, when she asked. "I was going to keep that for another tour, but we can go for a quick walk around now. We won't see much of the speakers. This is the time of day when they're off getting exercise in the form of a walk, though it's more like watching dogs herd sheep because the speakers wander every which way no matter how we try . . ."

He opened the door, letting in more of the warming

breeze. A stone path led through the kitchen garden to a long building closer to the hill. As with the main house, this was formed of gray stones with large multi-paned windows facing out over the lake. Strong winds whipped across the sky, while gentler breezes played closer to the earth.

Pausing to glance behind, Augusta marveled at the labyrinthine halls and rooms that formed the house, and the other outbuildings arrayed behind it. She hadn't realized quite how large the complex was despite the long, winding tour.

George knocked on the plain door to the long dormitory, but opened it before anyone could respond—not that anyone did. It was empty of people, giving Augusta ample opportunity to take in the whole.

"I know what you're thinking." George sighed as he stood next to Augusta, a hand on her shoulder. "That this is worse than how we care for speakers at the Institute, and it is. But we've such a hard time keeping it even as plain and decent as this."

"I don't understand." Augusta slipped from under his hand and turned around and around.

The large chamber was as clean and organized as everywhere else, but contained much simpler materials. Eight bedsteads sat at regular intervals with iron frames rather than carved wood. The metal showed pits, patches, and signs of rust, apart from odd gray ribbons tied around each post. Plain white sheets covered the mattresses, with pillows at one end and blankets neatly folded at the other.

Walls whitewashed instead of painted, revealing places tinged with moldy green. The underlying plaster had crumbled here and there. Anywhere from one to five panes of glass in each window had a notable crack, in some cases missing chunks to let in air. Just as well, too, for the air was humid and musty.

No rugs or anything to cushion the stark stone floor, which had several drains installed over piping or cisterns. A white curtain hung from a pipe attached to the ceiling, pulled to one side but the bulky folds appeared capable of forming a dividing wall if pulled across.

The wall facing the hill had two small bathrooms, each fully open to view despite depressions in the molding indicating there had been doors once upon a time. The toilets and basins were porcelain and clean, but the metal pipes and faucets showed the same rust as the bedsteads. The one interior door remaining in the wall was closed.

"We have so much more moisture here with all the water spirits—and the less water speakers communicate with humans, the more elemental spirits seem to come by. Too many rainstorms inside to count, day after day and week after week. We're constantly battling rust and rot." George pointed at the peeling plaster and rust. "Then there are the breezes attracted to the air spirits, they blow everything, so we try to keep things nailed down or tied down, or tucked away." He nodded at the closed door.

Augusta licked her lips, tasting a hint of mildew. The constant presence of air and water spirits was one reason the third floor of the Institute remained plain, if not so much as this. Yet they had so much less in the way of mold or rot or rust, even though they housed speakers losing the ability to talk to humans.

After which, they were sent here—and things got worse?

She peered into the bathrooms, noting the soft, intermittent drips from the taps and the tinge of green in the grout around the shower tiles.

"We can't trust the speakers to remember to do anything," George said. "They must be escorted and reminded constantly—have they eaten? Drunk? Used the toilets? We've given up on pants—that was one of the first changes the staff suggested—so now we give them all long smocks."

As Augusta turned around, the ribbons decorating the bedsteads caught her eye. Except, when she drew closer, they proved to be thick cords, with heavy rusted clips at the end. Puzzling, until she glimpsed movement out the window. She stepped closer to get a clearer view.

Servants in dark-gray outfits—uniforms, not livery—did indeed herd a group of seven speakers in long white smocks. The servants showed signs of impatience, tugging on one here and giving a push there. The speakers' feet were bare, or maybe they wore sandals? They formed a jagged line, lurching at different speeds as breezes twined around some while small rainclouds attended others.

Each and every speaker had shackles of gray metal in various stages of rusting around their wrists and ankles, and around their waists . . . Augusta whirled around to stare at George. "They're chained?"

"Of course they are." He ran a hand through his hair, grimacing. "Do you know what happens to speakers if we leave them loose?"

"They walk around."

"Oh, no. Not speakers such as these, who have given up communicating with other people." George shook his head. "When unchained, the water speakers ran down to the lake, right in over their heads, and vanished. Winds swoop down and snatch air speakers if they're not tied down. We lost so many—I don't want to think about the number—to the water and winds before we learned to take better care. We never did find the bodies—not the air speakers and not the water either. Do you know how hard that is on a family? They entrust their relatives to us and then we have to say they've vanished. Telling people their loved ones are dead is easier than that they've disappeared."

Augusta flinched, as though she'd petted a cat backward against the lay of hair, remembering the years of meals spent with empty chairs serving as a reminder of people who might be alive and reluctant to return or dead and never knowing. Death was easier because it offered certainty—an end instead of repeated cycles of hope, disappointment, waiting, and wondering.

George took Augusta's arm and gently led her back to the house, passing a large scorch mark. Blackened stones had cracked under heat, although it was long enough ago that green plants had begun to push up in the gaps.

"I don't know what the earth does to its speakers, as we haven't had any of those here, yet." George pointed at the mark. "But fire consumes its speakers."

Augusta glanced back at the speakers being shooed into one end of the building. George's hand on her arm urged her on.

"We do our best to treat them with kindness," he sighed. "I'll show you more next time. But there's only so much we can do. They've chosen the elements, not their family and not humanity."

Yes, but the means he and his assistants chose gave Augusta the first inklings of why her mother fled. What Augusta's cousin and siblings would choose she wasn't sure, but her mother would definitely have preferred their lives, however long or short, not involve chains.

Deep in Augusta's bones the word *wrong* reverberated

over and over. A half-dozen times, she opened her mouth to protest.

Yet by the time they reached the house, her memories of the tour blurred into simple relief that George and his staff cared for the speakers with kindness.

PART TWO
LUELLA TOBIE

CHAPTER 8
THE LOST COIN

More than anything, Luella Tobie wanted to go home. Nowhere else so much as smelled right, or had decent weather, on top of her missing her family and friends.

Baltimoreans considered this the start of summer, but not Luella. It was not nearly warm enough. She clutched at the fringe of her shawl, layered over a dark blue blouse with full-length sleeves and a high collar still tight around her throat despite her cousin May having adjusted it over and over. The older woman had finally thrown up her hands and accused Luella of not even trying to adjust to city fashions, even though as a fifteen-year old she'd have had to shift to dressing as an adult soon anyway. The shawl completely covered her single string of beads, which she'd brought with her and always wore. Her skirt-pants, color almost matching the blouse, had long, flowing lengths of fabric that allowed cool drafts to creep up her legs. Even her feet, wrapped in thick socks and stuffed into cramped boots instead of being bare or slipped into sandals, were cold.

Only the top of her head was warm, thanks to thick braids piled high.

If only she had speaking magic and could lure a warm air elemental to stay by her side.

Locals called this temperate weather, but it was too dry with not enough moisture in the air. Dry patches on her hands lightened from her usual russet undertones. On the other hand, her long hair needed less frequent oiling than usual no matter how often she wrapped it into a massive chignon.

Then there was the horror of her surroundings. Being in a city meant too many buildings all fixed in place with the ground underneath barely moving.

So much gray and not enough greens, and the browns were all wrong; dull slabs of smoothed stone or wood rather than textured bark and vibrant soils. Too few trees, all puny and wilted, instead of the Little Bird lands in the Seminole Nation-state with glades and gardens and fields and lots, lots, lots of trees where she'd grown up.

Nettee and Luella's other local cousins kept saying she'd get used to the narrow streets choked with dust and autowagons that made the most horrendous blaating sound when they steamed up behind her and their drivers wanted her out of their way. How long since the cousins had gone north? Or had their mothers moved first and birthed them here so they didn't know what they were missing?

Luella hadn't paid enough attention to who was related to who and had moved where when. Not the cousins in the first town or the city after that or this one, no matter that they'd been here six months. She couldn't ask now when she was supposed to know. May, her traveling companion —and the person supposed to keep her out of trouble because the chiefs and clan mothers didn't believe Luella could manage it alone, and considered her young to be off on her own—would no doubt take that as another sign to keep them traveling.

Six months. Nowhere near long enough for a girl to get used to straight streets lined with tall stone buildings. To learn to breathe despite the press of people thronging the streets and living in rooms overhead and speaking in strange sounds. To adjust to the unending shop fronts showing odd things she'd no idea what to do with—but no alligator meat or swamp cabbage, and while cousins had prepared boiled sofk with canned corn in the spring, it hadn't tasted quite right though she'd smiled and drunk it and longed for home.

She'd learned to find her way around some, though she rarely went alone far from the boarding rooms shared with the cousins. Every time she left May made her go over an ever-longer list of don'ts and be carefuls. At least this time, Luella had a nice finding fee in her pocket, thumping against her thigh as she moved.

This street she'd walked down enough times to begin noticing the blurry line where Chinatown ended—most easily marked by a restaurant, with bright red-and-white striped awning over the front and to either side of the double door, matching red banners with Chinese characters in white. A narrow stairway and door just beyond probably led to an apartment above. Wider stairs indicated the series of rowhouses beyond.

Early in the evening, lots of people sat out on the stairs talking in languages Luella didn't know or recognize. Probably Chinese, given where she was, but some words were Spanish or English, as most residents spoke at least a little of one or the other, but so many different tones and sounds with little to nothing similar to Mikasuki. So far north, only the cousins spoke that and not all of them very well—except, of course, May.

An older Black woman, part of a cluster on the far side of the street, waved to Luella. A week earlier, Luella had helped the other track down a missing child—an easy matter, for the baby had simply crawled under one of the wooden stairways and fallen asleep. Farther down, a young Chinese woman also smiled and nodded. Luella had found an earring for her, lost for ages but all the time stuck out of the way between two floorboards under a table.

Most findings wound up being that simple. Things lost, things misplaced, things left behind and forgotten. The closer Luella came to her current home, the more familiar the territory was and the harder for her not to notice what had changed.

Anything lost or out-of-place tugged at her as points of warmth despite the chill. A mangy once-white stuffed rabbit to one side of a stairway; no need to alert them as the child or parents would find it soon enough. A stray pepper had fallen out of someone's shopping bag an hour or two before, but was covered with enough dust Luella easily resisted the urge to scoop it up.

May asked Luella every evening about how many lost things she'd picked up. Stupid though it was, Luella got smilies inside when she was able to say she'd let things lay where they were—save for those lost so long the connection to whoever'd owned them was gone, and even *those* only when they were worth money or could be put to good use.

Especially since not letting things lie—or, worse, returning them to their owners and telling them exactly where and how they'd gotten lost—had landed her in trouble on too many occasions. Hence her current wander-ings until certain chiefs or clan mothers—or both—stopped being mad at her.

An old Chinese couple squatted on a stoop near the end, frail and thin, in matching red tunics with black embroi-dery at the sleeves and high collars over gray pants. The husband's scraggly white beard spilled half-way over his front. His wife's gray curls nearly matched the silvery trim on her curved slippers. They were there every evening in good weather, leaning close and rarely smiling or reacting to anything on the street.

Only once had Luella seen any signs of animation—a few days earlier when she'd found a little bronze bell in a pile of dust sweepings at the edge of the street. A tiny thing, she could have hid the whole in her hand with space to spare. Lost, of course, but she'd felt the warmth, the pull, and scooped it up knowing it belonged to them.

They'd been happier than she'd imagined. Chattered away in a mix of Chinese and English, until a young man came out to see what the fuss was. A handsome young man Luella's height with straight black hair and dark-brown eyes, so cute she'd snuck side glances while trying to pretend it didn't matter and hoping her heated cheeks didn't give her away. The couple's grandson explained it was an heirloom and that they insisted on providing a reward, especially when he told them she was a finder. The pineapple he'd retrieved from the house had been fine eating.

The couple clapped their hands and waved at Luella. She smiled and nodded, scanning the stoop and the door and windows in hopes of seeing the grandson, but no luck.

Around the corner, her cousins' stoop was nearly full of people.

May stood at the back, leaning against the doorway, a half-dozen or more bead necklaces jingling around her neck. Her yellow blouse and green skirt-pants stood out against the white paint and red bricks. She liked bright colors, saying people often overlooked her otherwise because she was so middling—middle height, middling brown hair and slightly lighter skin, middling features. Probably waiting for Luella to make sure she hadn't brought too many lost things home with her, unless they would bring enough at the small traders to make it worthwhile.

Sitting on the stoop, Nettee ruled in a long bronze-toned gown, queenly in height and size and with deep, blue-black skin and silver-tinged curls. Nearly a dozen bead necklaces hung around her neck, at least one more than May had. Nettee was the oldest of the local cousins, all of whom were from the Little Panther clan. May and Luella called them all cousins, aunts, and uncles.

The third was a stranger—a small woman in a blue tunic over gray skirt-pants. Her hands clutched a large black bag on her lap. Likely no taller than Luella's shoulder if she were to stand up, she had straight black hair cut short and dark-brown eyes, just as the old Chinese couple's grandson had. This was too near Chinatown to be sure the stranger was a relation, but so soon after Luella had found the bell, she was sure there was a connection.

"Ah, Luella, you're back safe!" Nettie's deep, resonant tones rang out, then she waved at the stranger. "This is our cousin, Luella Tobie, Little Bird clan, up from the Seminole Nation bordering Florida. Luella, Wang Ai, Mrs. Wang, a neighbor."

"Miss Tobie, a pleasure to meet you. You are a pathwalker, I hear?" Mrs. Wang smiled, but the expression of her eyes didn't match—too focused on Luella.

Luella stopped in the middle of the sidewalk, hands clenching and spine stiff. There were few enough out walking to make it safe. The three on the stoop had left room open to pass through, but she'd have to brush by them and she knew better.

"Is that the right word?" Mrs. Wang must have noticed Luella's reaction, for she frowned and tilted her head. "Waywalker? Finder? Pathfinder?"

"Hunter, spotter, discoverer." May offered a few more options in her light, breathy voice.

"I prefer finder," Luella said. The sweet smell of chicken roasting floated from the back of the house, maybe with the last of the pineapple in the sauce? If so, worth pushing through. Her stomach rumbled.

"Not pathwalker? That is most popular here." Mrs. Wang nodded in either direction.

"Pathwalker must've been dreamed up by someone who belived that once a finder starts finding things—sets foot on the path of finding—they can't ever step off." May clicked her tongue. "I like discoverer, myself."

"Finder is fine. It's what I do." Luella shifted her weight, feet aching from standing on the hard surface.

"So don't call her a pathwalker." Nettee patted the space between her and Mrs. Wang.

Luella eased down, the back of her neck prickling due to May standing behind. She kept her voice light, but maybe some frustration seeped through. "Why should I—anyone —have to spend their life wandering some magical path just because a person used magic to find something before they knew any better?"

"You've hardly wandered much yet," May muttered, but soft enough Luella could pretend not to hear her.

"Isn't it worth it? To know where things are?" Nettee heaved a big sigh. "I wish I had some powers."

"Every magic comes with pain and price." Mrs. Wang pursed her lips.

Something in her voice struck Luella as having a more direct understanding than most. The only way to know was to ask. "Are you . . . ?"

Mrs. Wang shook her head. "My brother. Younger brother. He speaks with spirits of earth and air."

She fumbled opening the bag on her lap, then pulled out a small photo in a light wood frame. It fit easily on her hand as she held it out.

Luella couldn't not look at it. Her polite glance turned into something longer as the image caught her. A man slightly younger than Mrs. Wang looked out on the world. They shared the same deep eyes in round faces framed by fine dark hair cut short. He had a wider nose, and a thin, wispy mustache and beard. But probably the first thing anyone would notice—certainly where Luella's gaze went—was the small shock of hair standing straight out from one side of his head. That, and the amusement on his lips and the way his eyes both looked to the side and gazed nowhere.

"He looks nice. He speaks to spirits, does he also talk to people?" The same kind of people who shared stories about finders condemned to be ever on the move also whispered that sooner or later folk who spoke with the elements had to decide between communicating with spirits or with humans, and the elements almost always won. The only speakers Luella had met, even in passing, were Panther clan from a village west of her home.

"When he is here, he talks to us as much as the elements." She sighed as she passed the photo on for Nettee and May to view. "He is not often here, very much in demand. Last year, twelve months or so, he went to Scranton to work on making new flexible spars for railroads. He rarely writes letters, but sends word by wind spirit now and then. The winds do not always deliver his messages in order, or in good time. My husband does not hear, but my parents and my sons and I do. My sisters, too, and their children, all who share ancestors. A telegram came a few months ago that he'd gone to Albany, some matter of wind and fire, and then silence for months until . . . he didn't return for Tomb-Sweeping Day, but a wind blew through us all with one word."

She paused, gaze fixed on Luella.

Luella's shoulders tensed, an ache spreading down her back. She'd found a missing bell for the older couple—either they were Mrs. Wang's relations, or somehow Mrs. Wang had heard. Her appearance this evening had to be planned. Keeping her lips shut, Luella refused to give the visitor permission to continue.

One of the cousins was bound to, anyway. Nettee broke first, asking in a rumble, "What? What did the wind say?"

Mrs. Wang didn't shift her gaze away from Luella.

"'Help.'"

That was what he'd said, but also what Mrs. Wang wanted.

"I'm not that kind of a finder." Luella crossed her arms over her chest. "I don't fix on people and know where they are. Or places. I find things. Little stuff—missing rings and watches."

Sometimes Luella was hired to find things specifically, others times she'd just go walk and see what she could find of value, which was rather a lot in a city such as this, and either return items to their owners for reward or sell her findings.

Or run away when she found the wrong thing in the wrong place or returned it to the wrong person. She still didn't understand why people would sigh and sob and promise a reward for something they didn't actually want found.

"I've tried to hire pathwalkers—finders—but there aren't many of you, and even fewer good at finding people." Mrs. Wang slumped, head down and chin brushing her neck. "How do I know who is good? When they want payment up front to go and look?"

No word from behind, though May had plenty of opinions and rarely held back airing them. Worse, Luella caught May nudging Nettee with her foot, evidently mute indication to hold silent.

Which worked. Even filled with righteous irritation at their meddling, Luella couldn't manage to match their silence, even when her foot started tapping against the ground, the soft clicking not enough to break the quiet.

"Is there someone you want me to . . . check out? Tell you if they're any good?" Luella asked. "I'm not sure how I would know, but—"

"If there were someone, then yes that would be a kindness. There is not. Was not." Mrs. Wang shook her head, seeming to become even smaller. "Until you found Mother's bell.

All this because Luella had noticed a small piece of bronze at the edge of the road. Metal covered over with dust, true, to the point that no one would have any reason to disturb unless they knew there was something lost there.

"But there is this." Mrs. Wang pulled a piece of paper from her purse and thrust it under Luella's nose.

Luella grabbed it reflexively before noticing it had a drawing, not words. A large double circle, the lines thin and close together, with a small square at the center. Four sets of lines formed figures between the square and the inner circle. One resembled a fish while the others were just lines —but all of them had a vague familiarity. They were similar to or the same as the characters outside the restaurant one block over.

Energy rippled along her hands, down her arms, through her torso. Warmth flashed through her.

"It's a good luck coin, very old. My father's father's, passed through many ancestors." Mrs. Wang leaned close, heat and tension pouring off her. "My brother carried it always."

Luella had never seen a coin like this. She jerked as her magic affirmed there was nothing quite similar anywhere in Baltimore. Her fingers opened and she dropped the paper as though it were about to go up in flames.

It wafted through the air before Mrs. Wang snatched it.

Too late, because the image had entered Luella's mind —and magic. Power swirled out from her, seeking the coin. This one, only this one. She rubbed her temples as blood throbbed in her veins. Her magic noted similar coins but not close enough in various places.

"His name is Zhang Cheng, you would say Cheng Zhang. My parents are old and long to see him." Mrs. Wang held the drawing between them, as though it were a shield. "Please. Find him."

"How did you know?" Luella's muscles started to twitch with the need to be on the move. A pulse beat far to the north—the cold, chilly, unwelcoming north where the coin was.

"Know?" Mrs. Wang frowned, drawing back.

"To show me a drawing of something unique?" Luella's teeth chattered, but she got the words out.

Mrs. Wang didn't reply, but her gaze flickered at something behind Luella. Or someone.

Luella lurched to her feet, rubbing her arms. She stared at the street and the long lines of rowhouses and businesses, the place she'd just started to find her way around. She glanced at the kind, loving face of cousin Nettee whom Luella hadn't known before but had grown to care for. Noted, without looking directly at her, the twist of satisfaction of May's mouth.

All of which Luella would have to leave behind, except May.

May's fault—but also Luella's, because she'd found Mrs. Wang's mother's bell.

Mostly the fault of the stupid magic that flowed in Luella's veins for no known reason. Chance that it came to her, or her mother had slept with some passing stranger who left his blood behind in Luella, or whatever.

Too late for anything but do as her magic demanded and find the lost coin—and try desperately to figure out how to avoid getting caught like this again.

"I don't know where your brother is. I don't promise I'll find him or word of him." Luella leveled a calm look at Mrs. Wang, willing her to understand the limits of what Luella could and would do. Someday, somehow she'd figure how to deny the demand of magic, but not this day. She glared over Mrs. Wang's head at May. "But I can find the coin."

CHAPTER 9

FINDING ISN'T FREE

Luella followed May and Mrs. Wang up the stairs. Blood pulsed at her neck and wrists, and sweat made her shirt stick to her back. She pulled off her shawl and crumped it into a ball suitable for digging fingers into. Her belly kept rumbling at the sweet cooking smells filling the house. Half the stairs creaked, while the railing was sticky in spots and over-polished in others.

One of the younger cousins called from the kitchen at the back. Nettee called back about dinner being delayed, while thumping down the hall. She could be cool and calm, though she'd have to find someone else to let the room after May and Luella left.

Mrs. Wang could be calm since her trick had worked.

May could be calm because she'd been asking Luella about moving on, plus she got to make sure Mrs. Wang paid enough for the trip north to find the coin—which was all Luella would find. Mrs. Wang might do what she wanted with news of the coin's location if it wasn't in her brother's pocket when Luella and May caught up with it.

Under other circumstances, Luella enjoyed watching

May haggle. The older woman managed most people to a nicety. She'd quickly convinced Nettee to wait below and whisked Mrs. Wang and Luella inside to settle the details. Luella didn't know of any type of magic that explained May's knack, though she wished she did. She'd trade.

Then she'd be the one managing rather than being managed. Again. Always.

May evidently sensed Luella glaring, because she turned at the top of the stairs and laid a finger against her lips just when Mrs. Wang moved up, so the other woman wouldn't see.

And gave Luella back a sharp look of her own. Luella's presence was necessary, but not her voice, not until she placed a high value on her finding gift and sharpened her ability to bargain on her own behalf.

"Magic costs," May had told Luella before Luella got a reputation for finding things, as May was one of the first adults in the clan to notice. "Find easy things all you wish. Find for family and clan, those whom you love and who love you. Find in times of dire need when you wish to help. But do not find for free."

When Luella first left the village—was encouraged to leave because she'd found the wrong thing at the wrong time and said as much too many times, or so she preferred to believe—May volunteered to go along and watch over Luella. May also took on negotiating finding fees so they could support themselves on their travels through Luella's magic, supplemented with May's work as a seamstress. With each new city they visited, May raised the charges. People rarely denied her. They bargained, some harder than others, but always paid.

Because May made clear that if they didn't, Luella wouldn't work for them.

Something Luella couldn't say for herself yet without outright lying at least half the time. She couldn't this time either. Magic linked her to the coin, as though Luella were caught on a fishhook and being reeled in. Unless she someday figured out how to get off the hook, she *had* to find it. The only way she'd found so far involved fixating on finding something else instead, which didn't do anything about the problem of needing to find.

She'd picked up a book about famous finders, her first purchase once she'd earned enough, in hopes it would offer insight into how to handle her gift. Unfortunately, it mostly offered brief biographies of the most powerful and active finders of the past century, such as the Tangemans—uncle and niece who guided many of the second founders to the Reconstitutional Convention—and people from earlier times who might have been finders even if they weren't ever called that.

Luella had yet to find anything on finders that offered more than praise of the dead.

Certainly nothing in the books told her how to handle —or undo—when her gift fixed on finding a particular item. Already, she'd formed a link to the lost coin. She could insist on staying in Baltimore, but she'd be edgy and uncomfortable for however long it took for the need to find the coin to wear off. Better to let May negotiate, move on, and maybe *next* time avoid getting caught.

May led Luella and Mrs. Wang into the small room she and Luella shared. Two single beds snuggled along each side wall, both made up with well-mended sheets and a thin pillow at the top. A banged-up suitcase under each iron bedstead, and those an improvement on the thick paper and cord they'd used to wrap their possessions when they first left. A bureau and hard-backed chair with a woven-straw seat stood against the inside wall, a few framed prints of city life adorned the walls, and a rag rug covered the floor. A draft slipped through the open window, making Luella shiver as the air hit her damp back. She wrapped the shawl back around her shoulders, huddling in to keep warm.

A tidy space because they didn't have much. Everything they owned fit in their suitcases. They didn't have a trunk because they couldn't carry it if running to catch a train.

So many things she couldn't own or have or do, thanks to the need to *find*.

May gestured for Mrs. Wang to take the chair or choose a bed to sit on. She sat on the one on the right, raising barely a squeak. Her back was straight, but the hand holding the drawing shook. Maybe she wasn't so sure as she seemed.

The other bed gave a notable creak as May settled onto it.

Luella perched on the hard chair. Only after she'd sat, when it would be a no-no to pop right back up, did she realize she could see out the window to the north and east.

Such a different view, of alleys and more houses and the pink-tinged sky in the distance. So unlike her family home and even the other places she and May had stayed while zigzagging their way to Baltimore, but familiar now and dear because she had to leave and go farther north.

"Luella will do all she can, but this will not be easy." May clasped her hands, her usual beginning to negotiations. "We will need money for expenses."

"Yes, yes." Mrs. Wang nodded, tucking the drawing back into her purse and holding on tight with both hands. "All will be arranged—trains, rooms, meals, and a reward for success."

"We don't know where we're going, or how long it will take to get there, other than . . ." May turned to Luella, eyebrows raised.

"North." Luella frowned and checked the alignment of the tug, using the landmarks outside the window. "And east."

"That leaves so many places." May sighed. "The coin could even be somewhere in the ocean, on a ship, perhaps."

"No, never. Water spirits dislike my brother. Made him very sick when we came to this country. Tried to drown him once." Mrs. Wang shook her head. "He would never go on the ocean."

"The coin may not be with him," May said.

"He would not give it up."

"I'm sorry to say this, but someone might have taken it from him." May set her hands on her thighs and leaned forward. "We cannot guarantee anything except that, if we can agree on terms, we will find the coin."

Oh no, Luella would find the coin whether or not they came to terms. The connection between them had already become so strong she couldn't imagine it wearing off. Object though the coin was, it wanted to be found, or some power wanted it found. Her arms pressed tight against her sides, legs together. It was all she could do not to pull her knees against her chest. Something wrapped around her, covering every part. Even her face. Her vision grayed. She tried to open her mouth, but a sour glue-like taste bloomed on her tongue. A shiver dispelled the sensation, but the taste remained.

May flashed her a warning, unnecessary. Luella knew better than to speak.

Or do more than pay the barest attention as the two dickered over the fee for successfully finding the coin. But when May started to negotiate an advance against expenses, Mrs. Wang stood up.

"All expenses will be paid. There is only one thing left to arrange. If you permit?" She pulled the drawing from her purse and laid it on the bed. Glanced at Luella, then pulled out the photo and placed it beside the drawing. "I will be right back!"

Before May or Luella could protest, Mrs. Wang zipped through the door. Her light steps echoed down the stairs.

May watched with pursed lips. In a low voice, though Mrs. Wang was far enough away not to hear, she wondered aloud where the other woman was going, and why.

"What difference does it make?" Luella shifted to Mika-suki—a touch of home—as she crossed the room and grabbed the window sash. Beating back the urge to slam, she closed it gently. Better the still air and warmth than the draft—or a breeze spying. "If you didn't want us to go after the coin or her brother or whatever she told you, you shouldn't have told her how to catch me."

"What do you mean?" May asked.

"You told her to bring the drawing." Luella pointed at it.

Her cousin paused, tilted her head to the side while observing Luella, then shrugged. "I did it for you."

"For me?"

"You've been twitching and jumping at shadows these past days, well over a week. Finding little lost things no longer satisfies enough for you to settle. You're noticing everything around that's out-of-place—lost or missing—whether or not it's something anyone wants found." She brushed her hands and twined her fingers in her beads. "It's clear you've stayed here too long and need to be on the move again."

"I like it here." Luella sank down onto the vacated bed,

careful not to disturb drawing or photo. Both were etched in her brain regardless. The springs creaked under her weight.

"So do I, but liking a place and needing to move on are separate things."

Luella stamped, but the thick rag rug turned the gesture into a soft thud. *"You* want to go on."

"I will always want to see new places, meet new people." May nodded. "But I stayed with you in Savannah and Charleston for months, did I not? With never a word urging you to return to wandering. I said nothing here, either. Did nothing. Until it became clear you were dawdling no matter how twitchy you got, and a little push was required."

"I don't want this. You should have the . . . gift."

May rattled her beads, standing and sniffing the savory smells wafting up through the floorboards.

"I want to go home." Luella pulled her shawl closer, although she didn't need it as much with the window closed.

"We will. Someday."

"When?"

"When you can hold your tongue about what you find, for one thing." May squinted at Luella, shaking her head.

That long.

Luella wanted to blame her departure on having found a lone bead necklace left under a bed in the wrong house and returned it to its owner in front of others, and a few other such instances. Still, May's mentioning Luella getting twitchy and noticing everything was a good description of how she'd felt then.

May patted Luella's shoulder. "Someday we'll go back

with plenty of good stories to tell, about all the places we've seen and the different things you've found."

"But we won't stay. I won't be able to," Luella said, and didn't shut her mouth before more slipped out. "You don't even want to."

"Some of us enjoy seeing new places, meeting new people." May nodded.

"You could travel on your own."

"Earning my way with my needle?" Luella's cousin shook her head. "I tried once, years ago. I didn't get half as far as fast as we've gone together. Finding pays better than sewing. But best of all would be you only finding things when you want to. So find a way."

"Don't you think I've been trying?" Luella stood and whirled around. No matter how fast she went, she knew exactly which way the coin lay. She stopped, pointing northeast. "Thanks to you, I have to find the coin first."

May opened her mouth, then stopped at distant voices and a round of giggles. Feet thumped on the stairs, heavier than before though not running. At least two people climbing at a measured pace.

Luella shifted to stand side-by-side with May.

Mrs. Wang appeared in doorway followed by a young man older than Luella by a handful of years at most. A familiar young man about Luella's height, with similar features to Mrs. Wang. Smooth skin with light gold under-tones stretched over a round face with a thin nose. Straight black hair cut short, only a few shades darker than his deep purple tunic with its high collar. He wore wide-leg black pants and soft black shoes under. Setting his hands on his thighs, he bowed slightly.

"My second son will go with you, Wang Jun. Handle all

costs, make all arrangements." Mrs. Wang beamed as she introduced him. "You may call him Jun."

"With us . . ." May's mouth gaped as she spoke first in Mikasuki, then shifted to English.

"I'll send word when I find the coin." Luella flushed and glanced away when she realized Jun had caught her staring.

"This will be simpler." His voice was low and calm, and he spoke English with a soft drawl. "I can pay you the fee when you're successful, without your having to make a return trip or wait on the mail. After all, my uncle is unlikely to be willing to hand over his lucky coin to you even if you mention my mother's name. If I am with you, you won't need to obtain proof of locating him."

"What if your uncle doesn't have the coin anymore and I locate it but not him?" Luella asked, twitching to keep away a repeat experience of feeling wrapped head to toe.

"You get paid and I at least have a trail to follow to find him. In that case, perhaps we can come to an arrangement for you to continue helping."

"You'll be covering all expenses?" May asked, eyeing mother and son.

Mrs. Wang moved closer and started bargaining with May over likely costs.

Luella backed toward the window, glancing sideways at Jun. He followed, scooping up the documents his mother had left. Although he barely paused over the photo, he traced the drawing with quick gestures.

"Did you draw it?" Luella asked.

Jun nodded.

"And you're willing to drop everything to go with us? If they agree,"—she jerked her head in their direction—"we'll likely be off tomorrow or the day after at the latest."

"It's summer, so I'm out of classes, and my brothers can help my parents with the restaurant. It won't be the first time I've traveled north, and to find my uncle I would do almost anything." His gaze flicked discreetly over her, head to toe, but twitch of his lips suggested he knew she noticed. "Even if it didn't involve traveling with such lovely company."

Her cheeks warmed. She'd be traveling with someone besides May—a man, a young attractive man, and not a relation. Though she wasn't fool enough to think it would become anything. Still . . . finding wasn't free, but maybe this once it brought an unexpected benefit?

CHAPTER 10

CHOICES OF CONTROL

All expenses paid meant riding in the same passenger cars as everyone else heading to New York City or beyond. It was only half-full, so they had the front section of the car to themselves. Jun carried a covered basket from which emanated interesting smells of meat and pastry. Nettee had sent May and Luella off with provisions, too. Luella contented herself with a slice of leftover pineapple-tinged chicken. She dribbled water over her fingers with care, but scattered drops as the train rattled over a bumpy stretch. Wiping her fingers on a clean rag, she sat back to gaze out the window.

The sides of the car were well-polished wood panels, all light enough to show where cleaners had been unable to remove finger and palm prints. Sturdy green-and-gray plaid fabric covered the cushioned seats and backs, smelling of musty wool where she'd spilled some drops, especially where sunlight touched it. She sat as much in the light as possible, for the warmth. Her gray suit fit in well with the seat cover, the skirt-pants in the shadow practically the same shade as the plaid stripes. Her blouse was a lighter shade of gray, hair in her usual chignon, and the only spot of color her yellow beads. Next to her, May rattled with her many necklaces over her suit of dark brown. Jun, too, had opted for a fine suit of a lighter brown.

The railway car was fifth in line, just far enough as the train rounded a curve to catch occasional glimpses of the water tank right behind the engine. Water spirits took turns sending the train sailing along its course over marshes and bridges and through small villages. The world outside the window turned to a blur unless one watched with care. The wheels clacked away beneath them, rolling over smooth stretches of rails and bumpy ones where the binding between earth and rail had frayed.

Jun mentioned once or twice or three times that his uncle was working on developing flexible rails that could adapt to more movement than the current, maybe even extend or retract as necessary. He watched Luella's face each time, but what he was looking for she didn't know. For her to declare she'd suddenly managed to track the man rather than the missing coin? After the third reference, he dropped the matter with the result they sat in silence for a while.

Luella craned her neck to watch Baltimore disappear into the distance. She wouldn't miss the crowds. Living there had not made her fond of cities, but she'd liked the cousins and getting to know her way around. It hurt to meet and spend time with folk for months and then move on without knowing if she'd ever see them again. She'd write, maybe, though her handwriting wasn't too good—nowhere near May's—and they'd do the same, if they could figure out where to send their letters when she couldn't say where she'd be in one, three, or six months. May had managed it so far, so Luella *could.*

The silence weighed on her. Part of the reason she hadn't answered Jun's mentions of his uncle was her tongue tangling in her mouth making it hard to speak. Hard to look directly at him, too, especially risking getting caught looking. Easier to angle herself as though she wanted to only look out window, but positioned so she could watch him out of the corners of her eyes.

May, at least, seemed happy. Though she perched with Luella between her and the wall, she watched the views through the windows and pointed out every time the train passed something interesting—a tall church steeple, the remnants of an abandoned village, or a particularly lovely water scene as they crossed a small bay.

Across from them on the rear-facing seat, Jun also noted view after view. More than that, he'd pulled out a sketchbook and pencil and managed to make drawing after drawing with little need for erasure despite the unpredictable bumps and patches of rough rails. Even glanced at upside-down on his lap, Luella found them incredibly detailed and far lovelier than the sketch of the coin. He often added lines of text or Chinese characters to the images.

May too was delighted by the drawings. She showed no signs of trouble talking with Jun, asking him about his interest in art and his studies at the university. Energy vibrated off her as she drank in every anecdote and droplet of information about the two years he'd already spent.

She also drew out his ambitions to work for the newspapers, traveling far and wide to report on events with articles and drawings. He'd already had several pieces in Chinese-language newspapers based on a series of visits to Chinatowns up and down the coast.

He traveled almost as much as May had always wanted to, and seemed to enjoy it even as she did.

Then again, the two of them could talk and smile and laugh about the joys of travel. They didn't have the pulsing tie to a missing item pulling them forward. A wordless sense of urgency running through their veins with the visceral need to find the coin soon, soon, soon.

Why? She knew where to find the coin—or at least which way to go and how far—not the owner. The coin wasn't even with the owner, of that she was sure.

May's comments of the day before, about Luella finding a way to control her finding, kept running through her head. She needed something to let her stop looking for things, to ease the need, or some kind of control. There had to be something she could do. She gritted her teeth against the longing to somehow fling herself across the kilometers between and find the coin and end the finding.

This was worse than the previous times she left town in a hurry to go finding, except for leaving home that first time. She still wished she'd taken time to reconsider and find a way to stay longer.

The awareness centered over her torso, shifting as the train took a curve.

She wrapped her fingers around the place where an invisible rope seemed to connect her to the coin far away. Only air brushed her skin; nothing else not even the slightest hint of power.

All the same, she gave a tug.

Pain. Her shoulder flared as though touched by fire. She let go, doubling over and rubbing her aching muscles.

"Luella, are you all right?" May laid an arm across Luella's shoulders. "Quick, water," she said to Jun.

With a rustle, he retrieved a cool glass bottle from his

basket and handed it to May, whose hand hovered in front of Luella.

"Here." Luella, grabbed the bottle and pressed it against her shoulder. The chill helped, or maybe it was the passage of time—moments or not—since she'd experimented.

Something that had worked. For a moment the connection between her and the distant coin had eased—and in that instant, awareness of things lost around her flooded through her. There shouldn't be anything. The train followed the bay shoreline through a section with no sign of human habitation anywhere. Nevertheless, thousands, millions of lost things impinged on her: trinkets, bits of crockery, foundation stones swamped by sand or weeds.

Her shoulder still ached, but she'd have to try it again, or something similar.

Maybe she *could* learn to control her power? Or decide when to stop looking for something, except how would she then start again?

She refused to explain to May or Jun, not there and then. "Later," she promised, meaning sometime when they weren't on a train, and maybe when she and May were alone. She didn't want to admit to Jun how little she knew about her ability, or that she was trying to find a way to not find his uncle's coin if she chose.

They pressed her, but stopped when Philadelphia loomed in the distance.

Luella didn't like the city at the first glance or second. As big or bigger than Baltimore, it was unfamiliar and noisy, with so many trains running along the tracks through the station, most carrying heavy freight but a few other passenger trains.

Enough people got on in Philadelphia that a young, well-dressed couple in matching suits of royal blue squeezed into the seat next to Jun as the last available space. It only worked because both were nearly as thin as they were tall, with light-skinned faces born to look down long noses. They clearly resented everything about the trip: the carriage's inferior upholstery, unsatisfactory cushions, inadequate seating, and worst of all having to share with folks who didn't know their place and couldn't take blatant hints to move to another car or at least squeeze three together so *they* could have a seat to themselves.

May's legs jiggled and nervous energy practically poured off her, her hands clenched on her skirts. Jun sat tall and straight and he gave them a cold once-over before studiously ignoring them. Luella had the easiest time. Being the farthest removed from the newcomers, she had only to pretend she didn't see their glances her way. They all had to smell them, though, for they wafted about in an almost-visible cloud of jasmine and sandalwood.

All the same, Luella would have gladly thrown them off the train if she'd had a chance, long before the railway conductor came through to check tickets. He'd started before Baltimore, so he already knew Luella, May, and Jun to nod to, a middle-aged man with a pale complexion and a paunch that stretched the brass buttons on his otherwise tidy green-and-brass uniform.

The couple unloaded complaint after complaint on him as he reviewed their ticket and punched in the appropriate place.

"Ma'am, sir, you may move if you wish, but I'm not asking anyone else to change seats just for being here first." The conductor spread his legs farther and bent his knees as the train took a sharp curve. "You want to travel in real style? Divide passengers into different classes? Run your own train. You're on the East Atlantic Passenger Special, and we have only one style of accommodations."

"Run our own train indeed." The man sniffed. "Do you know how much the charge is these days?"

"For upkeep on the rails? Or staying on good terms with the nations and territories and states along the way?" The conductor chuckled. "No charge is too small to do things right. Better than getting in trouble with one of *Them*." He pointed out the right-side window.

Oohs and aahs further down the carriage suggested he wasn't the only one who'd spotted something special. The train had gone far from the center of the city. A big billboard placed between a smooth road and the rails proclaimed the land ahead jointly administered by the Pennsylvania Shared-Territory Authority, the Lenni-Lenape Nation, and the New Jersey Reclamation Agency.

Just beyond it stood an immense female form as tall as the train—but made of ivy. The leaves and vines forming limbs and torso seethed as the woman watched the carriages roll by.

Deep-set eyes of flaring reds—dark hearts' blood to orange-tinted gold—glowed within the otherwise green-and-brown face. A burst of warmth flooded through Luella when the eyes met hers, as though she'd stood under the midday sun at the height of summer. May gasped, and across the way Jun muttered something in Chinese.

The seat back creaked as the couple pressed back, leaning as far away as they could.

"That's . . . *Them*?" May asked.

"One of *Them*, the folks who gave themselves to the deepest earth to give it a voice in our day and time. We don't see *her* too often, but sometimes another woman or a man show up round about a couple places along the line."

The conductor wiped sweat from his forehead with the back of a hand. "I had an old man passenger on this very route when I first rode the lines, one who'd been part of the Reconstitutional Convention after the Troubles, and he said that was just how they looked when they came and laid down what the earth would accept from humans."

As though she heard his words, the woman of ivy smiled, revealing sharp, pointed teeth of stone in shades of gray and white, a few streaked with rust—or blood.

"She's watching me!" The woman gave a choked squeal.

"She watches all of us." May huffed, though her elbow jogged Luella's side because she was shaking so much.

So was Luella, for that.

In an instant, the ivy folded in on itself and the woman vanished.

The couple stayed silent for a longtime. After a while, May offered them a chance to make nice and talk sense. They were subdued, but engaged in polite chitchat that Luella easily ignored. No need for her to join in.

Jun's pencil scratched at the paper as he sketched variations on the woman made of ivy.

Luella took the quiet space as a chance to try and control the pull toward the coin again. She located the invisible connection and tugged, this time slower and gentler.

Pain blossomed along her side, but dull and low enough to ignore for a bit. This time her senses overlapped to the point she imagined she was three people at once. One rode the rails, conscious of all the minute lost items around, especially bullets and arrowheads and bones. Another retained a pulsing connection to the northeast. Yet simultaneously, a vastness surrounded her—except for the sense that someone watched her.

Glancing out the window, she squeaked as a woman's face appeared in the trees and branches, with the same fire eyes and stone teeth as the ivy woman.

Luella let go of the connection, and the face vanished.

Shivers rippled through her. She pulled her shawl from May's basket with shaking hands and tucked it close around her. Maybe she should wait to experiment until she found the coin. Time enough to learn more then. Warmth seeped through her at the thought. No doubt due to a break in the trees that allowed sunlight through . . . or was it coincidence?

CHAPTER 11
ANOTHER FINDER

Luella relaxed against the cushions in another railway carriage as they left New York City, and good riddance. She'd sponged her travel suit the night before, although it wasn't quite as crisp as the day before. Another morning, another train but upholstered in deep blue. Jun and May's baskets held bought goodies, but otherwise it was much the same early morning start—just so much more comfortable moving away from the press of people and the city, and all the losses that Luella couldn't quite ignore even with the pull to find the coin continuing to pulse over her torso.

Plus, she hadn't slept well the previous night. It wasn't the hotel's fault. Jun had led them to a lovely place owned and run by people he knew and had stayed with on a previous visit. They even had a copy of his article about the New York Chinatown, complete with a print drawing he'd made of the hotel, not that Luella could read the Chinese characters, but she recognized the facade. The place was clean and conveniently located near the station. Dozens of restaurants lined the streets offering mouth-watering food, mostly Chinese. A nearby street vendor offered a semi-decent sofk, which should have helped. But the hotel beds had proved decidedly firm. Worse, Luella had spent the night dreaming that the woman in ivy was staring at her.

As the train picked up speed, a cold draft seeped through gaps around the window, whistling as it wound around Luella. She huddled in her shawl glaring at the overcast sky.

That was the main difference from the day before. Farther north, further from summer, and now no sun to give a little more warmth.

And their destination: Albany.

Instead of sketchbook, Jun pulled out a book of New York maps he'd picked up the day before and opened to Albany and its surrounding territories and nations. He didn't have to say anything as he laid it on his knees.

Luella's vision blurred, buildings and streets and traffic overlaying the lines on smooth paper. Following the tug, she stabbed a finger near the center of the city.

Then frowned, as a second, lesser pull drew her to point just off the edge of the map with her other hand.

"Which?" Jun asked, taking out a pencil and making light marks as she withdrew her fingers one at a time.

"Here." Luella tapped the city as the faint pull dissolved into nothing.

"Best to head there first, either way, as there doesn't seem to be a rail line to the other spot." May bent over, studying the marks.

"That sounds like a good plan. The maps are current." Jun checked the title page and frowned. "Well, two years old. We can ask the conductor if there are any lines north-west of Albany other than the continuation up to Montreal."

Except he didn't have the patience to wait and got up to stretch his legs, heading off toward the back of the train.

The cars slowed even as he left. The view out the window steadied into a small village. A real village with a cluster of houses and businesses partly surrounded by a forest. The houses were wrong, mostly brick and stone with heavy angled roofs—rather than a mix of chickees made of wood with platforms raised on stilts under thatched roofs that let the air currents through. The forest was wrong, too, lacking many of the trees she missed and full of others she couldn't put a name to. Still, she found it much more inviting than any of the cities she'd visited.

The train north proved less popular than that between Baltimore and New York City. She and May had the whole carriage to themselves, with Jun still somewhere at the back, until an older man shambled down the aisle and stopped nearby.

He turned just his head to look at them. Light-blue eyes twinkled in a long-nosed face with a full share of wrinkles and skin resembling a peach past prime. The hair atop his head was grizzled brown, as were his eyebrows, but the shadows along his cheeks and chin full gray. His dark-brown suit had lost any snappiness, assuming it had ever had any, and hung loose about his long, lean frame. The right elbow and left knee each had a patch applied in almost, but not quite the right color. Collar and cuffs were clean but showed faint rusty stains from a too-hot iron. He smelled of sweat and too-sweet lavender soap, and carried a half-full sack with a musty tang that nearly overrode the rest.

"Anyone sitting here, or you mind if I do?" The stranger gestured at the seats on the other side of the aisle.

"No, go right ahead." May nodded. She leaned back against cushions, body at ease with no sign of tension.

The man tucked his bag by the wall and took the backward-facing seat, angling himself so he could study them outright.

The hairs on the back of Luella's neck went stiff and the otherwise solid carriage floor seemed not-quite as solid beneath her feet. Colors around him—the tanned peach of his skin and brown of his suit—didn't match what she'd seen before for a moment, then settled back. It might have all been an illusion.

Except he snapped his fingers and gave a decisive nod. "I figured it out. You're like me, only you haven't gone and stepped on the path yet, have you?"

"Do we know you?" May straightened, spine stiff and feet firm on the floor.

"I never met either of you, sure, but maybe you seen me somewhere." He had a light, breathy voice as he stood, jerking as the train started up but managing a bow anyway. "Victor Stanton Jones, I was and am, though no one ever calls me anything but Vic anymore, or hey you. Sometimes Mr. Jones, but I don't much like the way most folks say it."

Bracing one hand on the top of the cushioned back, he offered his hand to May. She took it gingerly, watching him through narrowed eyes.

He winked at her, then stretched further and extended his hand to Luella. "I find places, how about you?"

"You're a finder?" She jumped at the shock of electricity when their hands met. Would have guessed it was just her, except he winced and rubbed his fingers as he pulled back.

"Finder, pathwalker, waymaker, whatever you want to call it, that I am." He settled back down on the opposite side, close enough to see and speak but too far to touch again.

Though she had no desire to do so. Did all finders strike sparks off each other when they met? That would be one way to figure out who else was like her . . . though he'd guessed before touching her.

"How did you know she's a finder?" May shifted so she partly blocked Luella's view of the stranger. Vic.

"You do this long enough, you get to know the look of people. I'm right more than wrong." Vic took a long look at May, with a sparkle suggesting he liked what he saw, then a tighter once-over of Jun as the younger man walked up the aisle and took his seat opposite May.

Jun introduced himself, and Vic gave him the same spiel he had Luella and May, words in the exact order, before continuing "maybe one of you got a touch of binding, but nothing more, and I wouldn't swear to that, but you,"—he nodded at Luella—"finding's popping all over you."

"Popping?" Luella frowned. There was nothing about him that popped, unless she counted the moment when the colors went odd and the way her hair had stood on end.

"Don't you get a sense when someone's finding things?" Vic asked.

"No," Luella said, "you're the first I've met."

"First pathwalker on your trail? You're young enough I can see that." He dug into his bag and pulled out an apple, polishing it on his sleeve. "There aren't that many of us, especially given the way we keep on the move. Hard on a family, unless everyone likes the packing up and setting out as much as the settling in, and never knowing where the next year'll take us in more ways than one. Not many of us make it. I didn't last five years staying in one place— though I tried, but my wife died and that was that—not that it isn't worth trying for if you ever get time and the inclination."

Luella's cheeks grew hot. She refused to look at Jun, or May, since every word out of his mouth echoed the kinds of warnings May had been dinning in her ears for months, that Luella would never be able to settle anywhere for long.

"You find places, you said." Jun tilted his head back. "What about people?

"Mostly no. If you're wanting someone in specific like, I'm not your man." Vic gave him another once-over. "But you want me to find a place with a certain kind of people in it—say friendly or with a blacksmith or doctor or such— you might tell me about it and maybe I can dream it up. And sometimes I get little hints—there's this other way of finding, you see, following signs and mystic stuff, that I don't do as much with as I should except when I can't miss it—which is why I'm on this train in this car. I was heading north anyway—been a while since I've had a stretch of good meals and sleeping in a nice bed, so I figured I'd head back to Albany and get myself taken care of for a while."

Before Luella or the others could ask any other ques- tions, the conductor arrived at their side. He nodded to the three of them, then turned and held out a hand for Vic's ticket.

"Give me a moment, I got it here somewhere." He patted over his pockets without sticking his hands in any of them. All the same, a piece of paper fluttered to the floor by his feet. He scooped it up and handed it over.

"What is this?" The conductor leaned back and held the paper up to the gray light through the window. It was a printed form with spidery writing filling in blanks.

"It's my voucher. Haven't you ever seen one before? The Whistle Institute, up in Albany, they'll pay for me." Vic said.

"This covers to Albany only, no stopping and getting off anywhere on the way." The conductor wagged a finger at Vic.

"I know the rules." Vic nodded. He waited until the conductor had passed on to the next car, then turned to Luella. "The folks at the Whistle Institute, they'd love you. They have these big ideas of figuring out everything there is to know about magic. Aren't many pathwalkers who'll stay around long, so they give us vouchers, see, promising to pay if we come back and let them poke and prod us and ask a million strange questions. They hardly ever answer any questions I put to them, though, because all they say over and over is that they don't yet know, well not in so many words, more like they say they don't have enough evidence yet. Is that where you're going? Thinking they'll tell you who and what you are?"

"I never heard of them." A place where they knew about magic—did they know how to stop it? Luella reached for the book of maps sitting next to Jun. He passed it over, and she paged through looking for Albany.

"They'll poke and prod her?" May patted Luella's knee. "Better stay far away."

"It's not that bad. They got women scientists to talk to the women with magic when it matters, about personal things and suchlike, and men to men same deal, and once a visitor, a binder I think, who didn't like being called man or woman though they only frowned whenever I asked them what they did want to be called. And that Mrs. O'Leary who runs the place no matter what the men in white collars think, she's got a right tender heart." Vic pulled out a knife and offered to divvy up a fresh, red apple.

They all crunched on slices for a while, before Vic finally

looked around at the three of them and asked "but if you're not going there, where are you heading?"

"Finding something." Luella scoured the Albany map, locating "Whistle" in tiny letters just about where she'd put her finger down earlier. "Because I have to." Because she couldn't figure out a way to stop, or hadn't yet.

"You aren't on the path yet, there's no *have to*." He waved a dismissive hand before biting into the apple again. "Just ignore the itches and they'll go away. It's not fun or comfy, but just keep in mind that you're more than your power, and it'll go away in the end. Unless it don't."

"What do you mean I'm not on the path?" Luella snapped the book shut and held it against her chest.

"I'm a pathwalker. I stepped on and won't ever get off, not that I'd want to, not since my wife died. You haven't stepped on yet." Vic shook his head. "Your power isn't focused—that's what the Institute'd say, and just about how."

"I have to find lost things. I know where they are, and the less I look the more I know." Luella's shawl dropped from her shoulders but she ignored the sudden chill. How dare he tell her she wasn't up to whatever mark he measured her by.

"She is driven—" May said.

Vic waved a hand again, but he leaned forward and stared right at Luella. "That's what we do, we find. Places for me, lost things for you. But there comes a time for us all —sometimes once, sometimes several times—when we get a choice. Either we step up and do more, or we don't, and if we keep not doing it, then we dwindle. A power's nothing if it's not used and you're not hardly using yours yet. Though you're young, too, so you've plenty of time."

"What kind of choice?" The words slipped out without

Luella's bidding. Memory of the vastness made her shiver and pull her shawl back up.

"Now or . . ." He turned his hands up and out. "You dwindle."

"That's no help." Luella rolled her eyes.

"That's all I can give you, and it's more than I've given the Institute, though I've answered their questions by the bucketload." Vic settled back, talking between bites of apple. "But too many of them scientists are too busy asking questions and not asking me what I think they should know, which I'm not telling them until they ask. Why lose a week or two of free meals and a nice clean bed?"

"You only stay there a week?" The shortness of the time was the one thing that most made her consider believing him about not having stepped on the path, whatever it was. She'd spent six months in Baltimore and as much time in other cities before. Unless how long she could stay somewhere was a matter of age, and she'd have to move more the older she got?

"A week or two, more if it's bad weather and I can handle the itch to get back on the move, or I get sick, but elsewise, yes. I'm on the path." He threw the core out the window, then thumped his chest. "And I've got me a calling to go and see what I can see, and do what I can that needs doing, before I move on. At which point I turn around and keep an eye out for storms. Last time I stopped, I got a glance northwards and it was all storm clouds and lightning strikes, which means trouble, and I go where there's trouble."

Wandering around looking for storms did not appeal to Luella at all. She glanced at her companions, hoping to see equal horror in them, but May only looked sad and tired and Jun thoughtful. "I'd rather dwindle."

"That's what I thought, once on a time, when I was young." Vic shrugged, a wistful expression shadowing his eyes.

Although the temperature hadn't changed a smidgeon, Luella stretched the shawl even tighter around her shoulders. That wouldn't be true for her.

CHAPTER 12

FOUND AND LOST

The weather in Albany wasn't any improvement when they arrived. Overcast skies and a hint of moisture in the air, although it wasn't raining. Warmer than Luella had expected, but not truly warm. Hustling, bustling people filled the massive gray stone station as they disembarked. So many people all talking at once and making it hard to think.

Her suitcases weighed more than they had at the start of the trip, the handles making ridges in her palms. She followed May and Jun through the crowds to an empty corner tucked away next to a news stand.

Should they check in at a hotel or track the coin first, back and forth the discussion went until Jun decided they'd put their luggage in storage and go in search of his uncle. "It's early enough in the day that we've time to find a hotel after."

Luella stayed quiet. Her legs straddled her suitcases, protecting them against being knocked or whisked away, as she massaged her aching hands. The coin pulled at her. As always, she could turn around blindfolded and point the correct direction—unless distracted by a faint tug of something else.

What could possibly lure her? She knew nothing of the area, or people, save those she'd traveled with.

Vendors hawking food wandered the high-ceilinged chamber. Some kind of roasted meat sold over in one corner, sweet popped corn in another, and ice-cold drinks further beyond. Despite the savory scents floating in the air, a bitter ashy taste bloomed in Luella's mouth.

A soft voice, deep and resonant as though containing multitudes, whispered in her head, *farther north,* but in Mikasuki. Who this far away knew that language other than her and May? But it wasn't May's voice.

She jerked, arms defensively pressed against her chest and shoulders hunched. No one nearby paid her any attention except May and Jun, and they barely glanced her way.

Then Vic stepped out from the crowd to stand before her, his bag slung over a shoulder and a half-smile lighting his face. "Still on the fence?"

"What do you want?" she asked.

"Lots of things." He shrugged. "Not that I'll get most of them. Though I wouldn't mind knowing which way you go when you make your choice. It's not so bad, being on the path. There's ways it makes finding easier and more rewarding, even if it does mean keeping on the move."

"Such as what?"

He sighed and switched his bag to the other shoulder.

What had he said about the Institute men's questions? That they asked what they thought they wanted to know, not what he could tell them. She tried again. "What would you want to know, if you hadn't stepped on the path yet?"

Bright approval shone in his eyes. "Many things. For one, you're more likely to meet up with others of our kind. Our paths are our own, but they cross often and even combine. Many of the big expeditions across the country over the last century were led by several pathwalkers."

Luella did not consider that a good thing, but waited in hopes he'd have more to offer.

"As well, it's a rare year I don't see at least five old friends, and make new. And that's on top of the path winding back to check on my family, not least for special occasions." He laughed and scratched his chin. "Last pass through my brother's town, I got off the train just in time to join in my oldest nephew's wedding procession winding down the street. I hadn't even known he was thinking of popping the question."

"You go home?" She blinked. The world didn't change, but a little of the tension in her shoulders rolled away. Though—arriving in time for a wedding he wasn't aware of didn't seem much of a trade versus getting to stay near family.

"I have no home but myself," he said, "but I see those I care about regularly."

"Anything else you'd want to know, if you were me?"

"On the path, you get signs that help you figure out what you're heading into, and what your options are. I go for storms, but that's me. You could head for calm seas and safe harbors." He stretched out a hand. "Good luck whichever way you walk, and just in case our ways don't cross soon."

They shook hands, his gentle squeeze feeling dry and crisp—because he left a card behind on her palm.

Before she could more than glance at the mix of print and handwritten lines, Vic had vanished into the crowd and

May and Jun were turning to her asking if she was ready to go find the coin.

Of course she was, the sooner the better. She tucked the card away as they checked their bags at the station and grabbed a quick meal. The taste of the pickled onions from her sandwich lingered as they headed out into the dusty street.

And immediately ran into trouble.

Luella could draw a straight line between herself and the coin, as the bird flew—but the city wasn't laid out to allow for that. She had to choose which streets to follow and none of them were straight. One seemed to go north-northeast, only to shift and head northeast instead without any easy way to turn head more north. Either they turned around and tried another street or kept on and tried to double back. Their zigzag progress took twice or three times as long as it should have if she could've gone straight —or if she'd been familiar with the city.

It was just another collection of tall buildings built too close together with too many people when she started. The one grocery store they passed had a smaller variety of fruits and vegetables for sale than in Baltimore, and still nothing of the foods she most missed from home. A nearby store had a barker outside offering air and water spirits for use in autowagons. Behind him lay bags of winds and bottles of rivulets. Another sold odds-and-ends with heavy coats hanging at the end of a rack of dresses—not something Luella ever wanted to need.

Even though she'd gotten used to walking around cities, her feet hurt by the time they'd tramped down a couple of streets. Her shoes cramped her toes, and the hard city surfaces had no give. The exercise did get her blood moving and warm her up to the point she carried her shawl over her arm.

As they moved farther away from the river, the shops put less on display outside. The exteriors became fancier, with elaborate lettering on windows. The buildings themselves were built close together, though not always sharing common walls, and the windows were small but open to catch breezes.

People thronged the streets, all talking so fast Luella rarely made out more than one or two words, even when they spoke English or Spanish. Many wore lightweight suits and even doffed their coats to walk around in their shirtsleeves, smiling up at the meager sun peeping through the clouds.

Jun held the book of maps open and occasionally checked landmarks in it. Each time, he dropped behind a few steps but caught up quickly. May alternated between walking behind and beside Luella, by now knowing well enough to keep quiet as Luella traced a twisting progress to a large building on the corner of two somewhat busy streets.

Solid bricks formed the front, with ornate decorations around the doors and windows. It was set back several feet from the street and surrounded by a wrought-iron fence. A discreet sign attached to the fence identified it as The Whistle Institute for the Study of Magic.

Luella checked the streets and the front of the house, finding no sign of Vic anywhere. For that matter, there was no one visible right around the Institute or through the windows. It wasn't the friendliest of places: too big, too tall, too fancy, especially with the fence gate shut.

"Is this where the coin is?" Jun took a step back, surveying the building.

"Yes."

The gate hinges creaked as he opened it and marched through. Luella glanced at May, then fell into step after and May behind her. Five stone steps led up to thick wooden double doors. Each bore a heavy iron knocker. Jun rapped twice.

After a few breaths, the righthand door swung open. A solid young man at least a decade older than Luella blocked the way in. He wore a bright blue tie fastened in a floppy style with a matching handkerchief in his breast pocket, which drew the eye away from his otherwise sober gray suit. His dark-brown hair was smoothed against his skull with citrus-scented pomade, and his skin pale but flushed at the cheeks.

He looked them over, eyes glazing, and pasted a wide smile on his face. "Tours are the first Saturday each month, between the hours of ten and four. No tours other times."

"I'm not here for a tour." Jun stuck his foot in the opening before the man could close the door. "You've got something of my uncle's, and I'd like it back."

"Your uncle?" The other man shook his head and blinked. "How would you . . . everything we have is legally purchased or given or entrusted to us. There must be some error."

"No, it's here. Luella?" Jun angled to glance at her.

"About there," Luella pointed toward the second floor. "Toward the back, I think."

"Let us in so we can find it, and you can watch. We won't touch anything not ours," Jun said. "And then we can discuss how it came into your possession."

"Find it . . ." The young man's eyes went wide as he took a longer look over Luella. His whole demeanor changed, energy and excitement practically spilling off him. "Are you a pathwalker?"

"I'm a finder," Luella said.

He waved off the difference with a flick of his hand. "Pleased to meet you. We're always happy when a pathwalker comes across our threshold. I'm Jake Deyo and you are most welcome here."

The door opened wide, letting them all enter. The interior was cooler than Luella had expected, and she quickly wrapped her shawl back around her shoulders. Brass lamps lit the room, leaving much in shadow compared to the outside. Luella blinked as her eyes adjusted. The light reflected off something scattered over the ornate wallpaper, making it hard to look anywhere straight on. A thick rug cushioned their feet, hushing the sounds of footsteps. There were two big sofas, but neither appeared to be used. A wide stairway of gleaming wood led to the second floor. The ceiling was high enough to allow a balcony on three sides.

"If you're bent on finding something here, we would be most grateful if you would let us watch?" Deyo clasped his hands together and beamed at her.

"I expected you would," Jun said, but gestured at her to agree or not.

Deyo wanting to watch made sense, but others? "It makes no difference to me."

"Excellent." Deyo touched something on the wall and bells rang out in the distance.

A moment later, a host of other young men and two slightly older women appeared along the balcony—with one or two light-brown faces among the many peering down. Two older men, one bearing a distinct resemblance to Deyo but without the bright blue tie and kerchief, ambled out of a door to one side. More people peeped down from the stairs up to the third floor, including at least two women around May's age.

Deyo coughed. "We have a pathwalker here looking for a lost item."

The next moment, everyone burst into the same fast speech as the people in the streets—but with clear excitement. Some clapped hands or cheered. One jumped up and down. Others started laying bets on which of the three strangers—Jun, May, or Luella—was the pathwalker and would there be any false starts.

This was not the usual reaction when Luella tracked items. People were usually, but not always, polite when she indicated something lost was in their house or on their property. They'd insist that it couldn't be there, there must be some mistake, but progress fairly quickly to oh very well go ahead and look if you must while making sure that if the lost thing was found it was clear they weren't responsible, it was an accident . . ..

"Don't they realize this means they have something here they shouldn't have?" May clicked her tongue. "Your mother said your uncle would never sell the coin."

"I've seen this before, especially at the university. Professors, scientists in particular, can get worked up over the oddest things." Jun shook his head.

The oldest man, who introduced himself as Cornelius Deyo—and the father of the younger Deyo—stepped forward and clapped for quiet. He turned to the three of them, clearly unsure who was the pathwalker, and stretched his hands out to either side. "Find away."

Luella faced the same problem as when walking the streets—navigating when the direct line to the coin went through walls. She started up the stairs, soles clicking against the wood and quickly drowned out as Jun, May, and the Institute staff followed her. The staff behind and those still lining the balconies whispered about how she hadn't hesitated whether or not to go up, and laid bets whether she'd stop at the second floor or continue to the third.

Distracting, but not why she hesitated at the top of the stairs. The coin was somewhere on the other side of a long wall, and she had no desire to wander this way and that with so many eyes on her.

"It's this way." She pointed. "A coin, wrapped in paper or fabric, with more paper or fabric around it and metal around that."

Most of the watchers pulled notebooks and pencils from somewhere and scratched away as they followed Luella's every step. Every breath. But in the end they wound up in a small windowless room lined with metal cabinets and piled boxes. Despite the clean floor and lack of dust, it had a mustiness that made May sneeze as she entered the room and she voluntarily remained outside. There was much pushing and shoving, because there wasn't room for many inside.

The cabinets were locked, so the watchers in the hall made way to allow through an older woman with her hair piled in a bun higher than Luella or May. The elder pulled out keys and unlocked the cabinet Luella indicated.

"This is where we keep the possessions of research subjects who aren't able to leave on their own, and don't have families come to take care of them," the older Deyo said. "We turn things over to the State after three years if no one comes to claim them."

"Whatever they're looking for hasn't been here three years. Three months at best." The key clinked as the woman turned it. "We cleared it out in spring and started filling it right back up."

Half-filled it was, with one side holding packages of various sizes all wrapped in brown paper and the other larger items including several pairs of boots and thick coats. All items and packages had neatly inscribed labels attached.

Luella picked up a mid-sized packet from atop the pile. The edges gave, softer to the touch than she'd expected, as she handed it to Jun. "The coin is in here."

More whispers from the halls, including demands from people who couldn't see to know what was happening.

Jun started to open the package, but agreed when the older Deyo asked him to move to a larger room so that everyone could see.

Still bemused by the general excitement, Luella followed the crowd into a large, well-lit workroom with a half-dozen mismatched chairs and desks and whitewashed walls.

Jun unwrapped the paper to reveal a pair of pants and a blue high-necked tunic embroidered in silver with strange curves and figures. At the center was a packet of papers, the top one attesting that Cheng Zhang was a citizen of the Reconstituted Union. An old brass coin fell from a pocket, a near-perfect match for the drawing Jun had done: partly worn but with intricate lines still visible.

"These are my uncle's." Jun scooped up the coin and held it and the tunic close as he scanned the crowd for Luella, and turned begging eyes on her. "You found the coin and his clothes, surely you can find him as well."

"No need." The older Deyo pulled the tag from the package. "These were Zhang Cheng's. We sent him off to

Sanctuary Hall just the other week. It won't take long to get him brought back here for you."

With that, tension slipped from Luella's shoulders and she leaned back against the doorway. The longest track of her finding career done. At least she wouldn't have to do that over, or deal with Jun's pleas to find his uncle when he knew she didn't find people.

CHAPTER 13
THE NEXT FINDING

Luella perched on a bed staring at nothing. The mattress was firm and comfortable beneath her, a thick blanket folded at the foot, and the hotel clerk had promised she'd find more blankets in the bottom drawer of the doublewide bureau sitting against the interior wall. Drizzling rain coated the window, turning the world outside to blurry gray—but for once the indoors was warm enough for Luella to hang her suit jacket on the bedpost and sit in her blouse and skirt-pants, shoes resting where she'd kicked them off inside the door, next to their suitcases. Soft yellow lamps cast light from a bureau and the table between beds.

In all, May had found a nice place to spend a night without any cousins or connections in the vicinity. A matching bed for her, narrow with a smooth-finished wood frame, lay across the small room and bright-colored prints of mountains and forests adorned the otherwise plain blue walls. The chamber even had its own basin for washing hands and teeth and anything else necessary, although the toilet and showers down the hall were shared with others.

Dinner could be purchased for a small sum in addition to the room charge, and already savory scents of barbecued beef wafted up from below.

Why wasn't Luella happy?

She'd found the coin. Earned the check that May had gone to deposit in their shared post office account. For once, May considered the city cool enough that she'd shown little interest in staying to see sights. There was nothing to stop them from heading south the next morning.

Yet nothing pleasant flooded through her at the thought. No joy or relief or even a sense of completion at the successful finding.

Rather, weariness settled over her as heavy as a thick blanket.

Where in the city would Jun stay while he waited for his uncle? If she left on the morning train, she'd never know the end of the story. Wouldn't see him again. Hadn't known him long or expected anything to happen—but for the ride north there'd been that frizzle of excitement in keeping company with him.

Until she'd gotten twitchy and decided she had to leave, she'd always assumed that she'd end up working a plot of land in the village, as others in her family did. Maybe bring in a bit of cash or goods to barter through finding or needle-work. Marry someone from another clan and raise a family.

Only to give up hope when she left. Half give up hope.

If Vic were right in what he'd said on the train, that Luella hadn't stepped on the path—she still could dwindle and have the life she'd expected. Or step on the path, and then be in constant motion? Meeting people and spending a few hours or days with them, as with Jun, and then moving on?

Yet the notion of dwindling scared as much as attracted. She'd always known what was around her, the locations of everything regardless of whether her mother or sisters had been messing with her things. She might lose that if she refused to step on the path.

But thinking wasn't doing her any good, only sending her round in circles with no answers.

Rising, she retrieved her suitcase. A few remaining raindrops beaded on the waterproofed fabric. Blotting them on her sleeve, she set the case on her bed. She didn't need much, her nightgown and hair wrap and a fresh blouse and underthings for the next day. She always packed the same way, so they should be the first things she saw on opening it—and they were, but with something else atop them.

Vic's business card. Hadn't she put that in a pocket? Patting her skirt-pants, she found a second rectangle of hard paper. A sharp corner scratched her palm as she pulled it out to set beside the first.

The two were almost identical: on one side he'd written in spidery handwriting varying only slightly in angles and curves: 'In case you step on the path and are interested in regular work and a reliable stipend.'

The reverse had a printed inscription identifying Victor Stanton Jones as an agent for the Federal Bureau of Magical Investigations.

Rubbing the sore spot on her hand, she walked barefoot across the smooth, warm wood floor to gaze out the window. The rain turned the view into a blurry mass of gray sky and gray and brown buildings, with bits of green here and there where trees branched up from the sidewalk.

She couldn't see the Institute, although it should be to the left and several blocks away. The coin didn't seem to be there but a little farther away and farther west, though how should she tell? It wasn't lost anymore.

Vic had declared himself headed to the Institute for a week of clean sheets and solid food in trade for answering questions about being a finder. Now she better understood how much the scientists hungered for information, and that they'd welcome him with open arms. They'd do the same for her if she went back.

Still, the card changed things. Was he there for other reasons, maybe something illegal going on?

Did his being there, as an agent, mean Jun was in danger or his uncle?

What could she do? Track down Jun and give warning—though Vic had snuck her the card without giving one to Jun—and warn him of what, anyway? If Jun were wise, he'd be weighing words with care and not trusting anyone too much.

Should she and May have stayed with him until he reunited with his uncle?

So many questions and worries, of the kind she'd never had to consider before. Her head ached, blood pounding at her temples, by the time May returned.

Her cousin whirled in, smiling despite being wet head to toe. Almost. May wore a strange coat with a matching triangular hat, both in a bright yellow fabric that reflected the light from the lamps. It dripped, but when pulled off revealed May's hair remained dry and unfrizzled.

"I got one for you, too." May set a bag down and hung the coat and hat on hooks by the door. Underneath the coat, her clothes were damp at best, except for her shoes and stockings. "A store next to the post office sold them, and they're better than umbrellas."

"They'll be harder to pack."

"Oh no, the shopkeeper showed me they squeeze down delightfully. But that isn't even the best news." May dropped several bills and coins on Luella's bed. "A bit of spending money from the latest fee. The rest is in your account, except the monies we agreed to send home."

"Good news." And expected. Luella picked up the money and started stashing it throughout her clothes and suitcase, in interior pockets and linings.

"No, the news is there's a wonderful finding job for you, just the right thing, if you want." May pulled a folded paper from her hip pocket and opened it to reveal a printed flyer. "There were several of these, the clerk said they were put on the help wanted board only a few days ago."

Finder Wanted, the flyer blared. *Apply for more information with the Kanien'kehá:ka offices in the state house. Top dollar for success, time-paid for attempt.*

"How am I supposed to find something if they can't even describe it?" Luella squinted at the fine print detailing how applicants could find the offices, or enquire at a village somewhere outside the city.

"That's just for the flyer." May waved an airy hand as she squeezed her stockings over the basin. "It's probably valuable and they don't want to alert everyone and their cousin that it's been misplaced, or start some kind of treasure hunt."

"I suppose." Luella scooped May's dripping shoes and placed them over the heater vent. "It might be interesting to learn what they're looking for."

"The point isn't what you'd find for them, but who you'd work for. The Kanien'kehá:ka are one of the Haudenosaunee nations." May sat down, hands clasped. "This is exactly the kind of task that will lead to a wonderful story to share when we do go back."

"I thought you wanted to keep traveling, seeing new places." Luella returned to the bed she'd perched on, pushing far enough to lean against the wall.

"I would, yes, but that's not what you want. A poor cousin I'd be if I only cared for my wishes." May reached across the space between the beds to brush a finger against the flyer. "If you'd rather head south before taking another job, that's your choice, but I thought you might be interested." She paused for a moment, then lifted her eyebrows.

"I met up with Jun, as it happens, for he's settling into a rooming house near the post office." May smiled at Luella. "He'd like to take us to dinner tonight, as an additional thank you for your finding. I think he'd be as happy if it were only you at dinner, without me."

Jun wanted to see her again. A ripple of warmth from that ran through Luella as she read over the flyer again and again, all the while May chattered on.

The Institute leaders had promised to write immediately and have Jun's uncle brought to city at the earliest possibility, and Jun pledged to write a letter of recommendation for Luella's finding services, for the binder May kept. If May and Luella took the finding job, they could pass through Albany after and see how Jun and his uncle fared. Or even, if Luella was interested, talk to the Institute scientists about ways for Luella to control her powers.

The way the scientists had watched Luella's every movement as though it all had great meaning did not inspire her with confidence. But she might learn what brought Vic back to the Institute again. A tiny curl of curiosity unfolded within her at possibly learning what kind of work the other finder did.

Although, she remained uncertain as to what the Kanien'kehá:ka might want her to find. For a moment, eyes

of fire seemed to flare in the gloom outside the window—
and Luella rocked on her feet as though surrounded by
vastness and the least movement might lead to a fall.

But when she steadied and glanced at the window a
second time, only raindrops cascaded along the glass, and
the gray sky and buildings looked as they had before.

"Well?" May asked.

Find something unspecified for a local nation? Luella
might regret it, but there were good reasons to say yes. So
she did.

PART THREE
ZHANG CHENG

CHAPTER 14

WORDS

Cheng kept his eyes closed. His breathing remained slow and easy as he lay flat on his back on the thin mattress in the rickety iron bedstead. Fingers twitched, but surely that happened in sleep and would give no one a sign of his waking. If anyone watched. Sometimes yes, sometimes no, though he could not swear to no. Three, four, five days in captivity—had he lost count already?—and he'd started to learn the rules of his new world.

The better to hope to break them and escape.

The metal bonds circling his wrists and ankles retained a chill, so too the cords chaining him to the wrought-iron bed frame. Likewise the soft breeze slipping across his body and tugging at the thin, scratchy wool blanket covering him had a morning freshness and a hint of dew. Little of smoke, or just the tang of a fire new-lit from somewhere nearby.

Dawn light sifted into the room, but Cheng pretended to sleep as the darkness of his closed eyes lessened and turned to gray lined with red.

A soft scuffling in a far corner, nails against the tile

floor. The breeze whisked away from him and returned with the brush of whiskers against the back of his hand followed by the softer pass of a tail. The musk of cat blew through him, then gone, followed by the flickering sensation of tiny feet and a longer, thinner, smaller tail.

A cat tracking a mouse.

Much as Cheng loved cats, he had more sympathy than ever for the mouse.

This night he had been spared dreams. Small mercy.

One of the others moaned. To his left, three beds over.

A whimper to the right.

Rustling, and the smell of some type of cheese.

Who else was in the room? The kind breeze whipped around and returned. It swept the sensation of soft cotton across his arm and torso, and then brushed his tongue with the tang of eggs mixed with cheese. It was not something he would have chosen to eat, and he couldn't hold back a shudder.

Then froze. Had the movement been noted?

It didn't matter. Metal clanged against metal.

"Wake up." English words, always and only. Accents sharp and hard.

It took him a moment to adjust. Alone at night, he thought in the Shanghainese dialect of his birthplace. Elementals didn't notice. They comprehended meanings, not sounds—although breezes enjoyed taking his words, whatever language he used, and recreating the syllables as they danced. He'd smiled when they first started doing so, not then realizing it was the beginning of the end. That they might come ever closer until they stole his voice as he spoke. Or was it earth spirits that had rendered him mute? Though earth spirits no longer talked to him so much. He didn't want to talk to fire.

He had to force himself to translate or to shift and think in English. It used to be easy, part of his morning routine to consider the day ahead and move to whichever language would best work. English for working on trains and railroads, or the pieces of French and Dutch he'd picked up after years in Pennsylvania. Chinese when at home with family.

"Get you up."

He didn't always understand each word, but the meanings came through.

More banging, followed by groans of protest or waking —but nothing understandable.

Cheng gave up the pretense of sleep. The walls looked no better in the soft morning light than the harsh midday. Once white, the paint had started peeling off in clumps— too much moisture in the air. Each and every one of the three windows—all west-facing, had at least one crack in the glass that let in stray breezes to snatch words from his and the other captives' throats. There were seven of them, four men and three women, all pale except for him and one of the women who had dark black skin and short, tight curls. A curtain of faded yellow and orange hung from a metal rod separating the men's bedsteads from the women's, but he'd never seen it pulled closed.

The stone floor was swept and mopped regularly, apart from the rivulets of water oozing from five of the others who were regularly attended by small clouds of fog—yet it never seemed to be clean. He, for one, appreciated the chance for his bare feet to come in contact with the dirt filling the gaps between stones, and the connection with earth elementals however small and incoherent.

"You next." A stout man with ruddy coloring and a short crown of rusty hair bent over Cheng. His white shirt and breeches exuded stale sweat, and his breath onions. Breezes whisked between them carrying away some of the scents, but even they could not spare Cheng from all.

The ends of the cord lashed Cheng's arms as the guards undid the bonds, but left the iron bracelets on his wrists and ankles. His remained steel gray against his fawn-colored skin, but others—those binding the water speakers—had begun to rust.

They gave him a loose robe to don. The well-washed fabric was thin in patches but still rubbed his skin the wrong way, especially the raw spots at ankles and wrists, but he knew better than to fight. Let them think him cowed.

He was the oldest, by far, of captives and guards. Even allowing for the difficulty he often had in guessing others' ages, all appeared to be in their twenties or thirties at the most. Only one seemed to speak with more than one type of elemental: the light-complexioned woman perhaps in her thirties about whom gusts danced with rain.

Cheng enjoyed the attention of air and earth. Water disliked him, at least in quantity. He had no trouble drinking the stale, watery oatmeal he was brought for breakfast. But since the age of five, he'd had to suffice with damp cloths to clean himself after the bathwater tried to drown him. He had a seed of fire in him, the one fire speaker he'd ever met said, and followed by advising him to let it lie.

Fire speakers rarely lived long. Word came of the fire speaker's death a bare three months later. He'd been twenty at best.

Cheng had followed the advice, or tried.

Air and earth, those were his gifts to speak with. To share some part of how he experienced the world, and receive in turn from them. At least he was no longer housed high on the third floor of the Institute. The very swiftness with which he lost his ability to speak with humans—the avidity of the breezes in taking his words direct from his throat—might be due to the extended separation from the earth.

Except, being back close to earth had not helped him regain his voice.

He should never have agreed to those last long months in Scranton, working with metals to create flexible rails. Metal was earth, but shaping it belonged to fire. Cheng's seed had sprouted, though it was still small and weak. He didn't speak with fire spirits, not now not ever. But sometimes he heard them in the distance—high above where lightning danced with wind—as they called him to join them.

The guard laid hard hands on Cheng's shoulders and turned him to face the toilet room, with its lack of a door so his captors could make certain he didn't escape or whatever else they thought he would try.

~How long have you been here?~ He asked the breezes to take his words to the other captives. His words emerged as whooshes, and whistles, the sounds of breezes.

Sometimes the breezes cooperated, but the smaller they were the less able to concentrate. He'd sent word to his family by winds over the years, and heard that they received at best a third of what he gave the winds to start.

Once he had spoken four languages well, and a fifth enough to understand and be understood. People hung upon his words, listened, and worked with him to bring ideas to reality.

Now—nothing.

A flicker of an eyelid here and there, suggesting maybe

one or two of the air speakers heard some part. But otherwise no response. They were one and all weakened. Arm and leg muscles thinning to the point they hung from bones. Gaunt faces.

Blank eyes and wandering gazes seeking . . . what? The air and water spirits circling around them unable to undo the metal or cords?

Perhaps they ignored the smaller elemental spirits, too busy listening to winds to bother with breezes.

This was his future. If he'd known, he'd have done so many things differently. Three or four times he'd heard fire speaking in the steam pits at Scranton, and each time after been unable to communicate with other humans for a matter of hours. The other inventors had worried over him. Taken up a collection from the railroad investors, and shipped him up to the Whistle Institute for evaluation and advice.

Some advice. The Institute scientists knew some things about speaking magic that he'd been unaware of, but they were as much in the dark as he, or more so—especially since they showed such little understanding of communicating with elementals in depth. At best some of them talked to a breeze or two, but rarely more. None, surely, had ever been embraced by a wind or uplifted by a joyous surge of earth.

And in going to the Institute, he'd lost the chance to go home. To see his father and mother one more time. To rest in the heart of family rather than among strangers.

Even before he was carried off to captivity.

He stood next to the rickety iron bedstead, with the blanket a lumpy mess at the bottom. Stared out through cracked windows at the hillside and the glint of water in the distance.

Breezes whistled in through the gaps in the glass, or

along the halls leading mostly to places he'd never been, likely would never go.

He called them, and they whirled around him. Shaping his mouth and throat, he gave voice to the sequence of pleas he'd uttered since the first night he was thrust into this horror. No sound escaped him, the winds saw to that, though the guards wouldn't understand even if they heard as he spoke in Chinese. They carried way his wishes for his parents' health and well-being, his warning of captivity outside of Albany, and his request for help.

If only the words might reach his family in good time.

These here, the guards and the man who commanded them, showed no idea of who he was.

They cared only what he could do for them—what they could make him do for them.

The kind breezes twined around his neck and along his arms, easing the aches and pains with their cool kisses.

~Go.~ Cheng told the breezes. ~Stay away until night.~

But he would need them, they protested in the way they caressed him. How else would he share the sensations of the world?

~Later. Not now. Danger here.~

The air resisted, breezes joining into a greater wind that ruffled the hem of his gown, whipped the edges of the blanket, and hissed at the guards. The other air speakers perked, turning their faces to the gusts with delight.

Drops of water splashed Cheng's face, as the winds' anger drew rain from one of the water speakers.

~Go!~ Cheng repeated. ~Stay safe. Do not return until night.~

The wind circled the room, knocking two of the water speakers back onto their beds. One crumpled into a ball of rain and fog.

Then the wind left, taking the other air speakers' breezes with it. Cheng feared it might return, as breezes and winds were often curious. If it didn't, there were sure to be others.

He followed orders to form a line, taking a place behind a rain-slick woman. The guards roped them together, wrists to wrists and ankles to ankles. She left damp footprints where she passed. A guard slipped in one and nearly fell.

Lashed out with his fist, knocking the woman forward and nearly clipping Cheng's jaw.

"Don't hurt them before they pony up," the other guard said. "They've got work to do. He'll see to that."

He—the man behind it all, the father not the son who was a pale shadow of his sire.

None of the others showed much in the way of fear. Maybe they were further gone than he, a warning of what might happen to him.

The blessing of the magic of speaking to elementals was the joy of sharing with beings pure and strange and other than one's self.

The curse of the magic of speaking to elementals was the more one listened to them, communicated with them, the harder it was to *not* listen. The more so as elementals spoke in so many different ways—and so many loved the humans who heard them in their full glory.

Increasingly, Cheng found it hard to hear humans through the great chorus of air or earth.

Or fire.

His ankles wobbled. The edge of his foot pressed against stone flattened and smoothed by the passage of humans, or by having been cut by humans from the earth. It didn't matter which. The mere fact that humans shaped the stone made it capable of fixing the earth on which it stood. Of denying the stone the ability to move—to rock or roll or turn about.

But it remained part of earth. Deep below, something stirred. A ripple of warmth flowed along his foot, followed by the softness of grass and flower petals.

~Safe~ The deep earth's assurance resonated in Cheng's bones. Although it didn't speak in words, the meaning came through. ~You are safe. We have you, we will keep you, guard you.~

~I'm not safe. Danger here for speakers. Help!~ Cheng sent back, but to no avail.

Over and over, the earth repeated promises of safety, as though it didn't hear him, though why then offer them?

A hard tap on his head broke the connection before he could try for answers.

He'd lost time. In the interval, he'd been brought to a small stone courtyard. A square, with walls all around save one side where wooden doors filled a rectangular opening. No roof overhead, so the cry of birds over the water echoed slightly, as did the not-so-distant chime of metal and voices. The stones here were fixed tightly together, with little dirt between. No communication welled up through them, leaving him as bereft of connection to earth as when he'd stayed on the third floor of the Institute. Water trickled through a pipe under the wall facing the far hillside. It dripped into a round depression at one side.

Cheng stayed away from it.

A great wind rushed high above, hurrying from west to east. Formed of a thousand or thousand-thousand breezes, the immense spirit paid little attention to the humans far below—but the edge of the it brushed Cheng in passing. Gusts filtered down and rumbled over the courtyard.

Smaller puffs whipped down and through the air around him.

~Go!~ He ordered. Pled.

One guard watched him, standing close enough to smell.

The other laid out canvas bags in circles around Cheng. Bag after bag, all open and empty.

For now.

Then He came. The first captor, the leader, Him. Neatly dressed in a light brown suit over his solid build, with a straw hat perched atop dark-brown hair. Deep brown eyes —lying eyes the color of warm earth—to either side of a long nose that twitched as though he'd smelled something nasty. Hardly much taller than Cheng, and likely much of an age, but more than capable of looking down upon him.

This time He came with a different shadow. Not the pale imitation that was his son, but a solid woman about his son's age. She had paler skin but the same color hair in short, bobbed curls and similar eyes, though set in a face empty of expression. A long, light green tunic fell to mid-thigh over split pants—and the hems of both fairly sizzled as an avid breeze tugged at her. Begged her to come away, though she showed no signs of noticing.

"Watch and learn," the first captor said to the woman.

Cheng tried to step back. The guard grabbed Cheng's wrists and held them tight against the curve of his spine. Cheng's body bowed with the effort to keep away from the man approaching him.

The first captor cupped Cheng's chin.

Dark eyes seemed to bore into Cheng, no matter how he tried to avoid them.

"Call the winds. Make them fill the bags for you."

The words wrapped around Cheng, but not the way air

elementals did. The command became chains squeezing his feet, then his legs, as though taking the form of a great serpent whose coils draw ever tighter as it moves higher. To his thighs, his belly.

His chest.

Air escaped his lungs. Seeped up his throat and out his mouth.

Little though he wanted, he obeyed.

~Come!~ Cheng commanded the breezes. Surely they'd hear the horror in him this time?

But gusts whipped downward. Breezes split from the great winds, which traveled onward little noticing for they were always growing and shrinking as breezes joined to become something bigger and separated again.

Bag after bag inflated and began to rise, as the breezes delighted in the game of lifting and tossing—never noticing that the first captor walked around pulling the bags closed and binding the spirits within.

The spirits Cheng lured down.

Twice more the guards arrayed empty bags around him, and fingers squeezed his chin with the command to lure the winds. One by the older man, the first captor, and once the younger, the son having arrived to follow in his father's steps.

Each time Cheng fought, resisted, but clenching bands around his belly forced him to call the air spirits.

How many times overall? How many commands and how many bags?

He did not, could not, remember. Only that one moment he stood in the courtyard counting up the straining bags of captive breezes—and the next he lay on the creaky bedstead under the scratchy blanket. A cloudy night sky allowed little light into the dark room. Cheng's belly rumbled, near empty.

He writhed, but he was once again tied to the bedstead.

How many nights had Cheng lain totting up the air elementals he'd betrayed—will he nil he—and trapped even as he was trapped?

The other speakers wept or moaned or snored in their sleep. They'd been here longer than he. Did they not care any more? Not hear him try to warn the breezes?

And why had none of them warned him?

Perhaps the first captor used his binding power on them. So many things blurred—time and hope and energy. Memories of his previous life faded. Lessened. Little existed but the here and now. That, too, might explain why his fellow captives no longer seemed to care.

If only Cheng's ability to call the winds slipped away, so he would not have to betray any more.

Or if the winds could stop his ears so that he couldn't hear the command, and hence not obey.

Or if he couldn't understand . . .

Somewhere in the buildings around there must be candles or sealing wax or bits of cotton, anything that he might use to stuff his ears. A poor trick, which might not work for long, but anything to give him more time to figure out a better way to resist.

To escape.

The night breezes came to play and tug at his blanket whip around his toes, then blast his ears with a dozen sounds some English, some other languages, and many not words at all.

It was worth asking. ~Can you find and bring me wax or cotton?~

The breezes turned around and around, briefly forming mini whirlwinds, but returned with puzzlement.

He formed image of wax and pushed it to the breezes, then cotton, but they were thin, small wisps of air. If he could have pointed to what he wanted, they would surely bring it to him, but lacked the focus to find it without help.

Until one breeze brought a thin stream of silvery luminescence behind it. Moonlight . . . except the night was overcast.

The luminescence expanded until a specter stood by his bedside. A woman in a shadowed gown with wide sleeves and immense skirts. Fine lace with points that glittered spread across her upper chest. A long, thin nose dominated her face. Though made of ghostly light, she bore a distant resemblance to the first captor, his son, and his woman assistant. The air around her lost heat, but the seed of fire deep within Cheng kept him warm.

The ghost bent over him and her lips moved, though not a sound did she make.

A breeze spoke with a woman's voice, carrying sounds to his ears in English.

~I will help you, if you wish. Guide the breezes to bring you what you ask for.~ She passed a ghostly hand across her lips and nose as the breezes whispered her words for her.

~What do you want in return?~ He shaped the words carefully, trying to speak but unable to make a sound, even as he shrank away inasmuch as his bonds allowed.

~Something simple and difficult. When you escape— ~

A creaky laugh escaped him, an actual sound that for once the breezes didn't whisk away. Escape? How much he longed too, but the surest way for him to get away was to die. ~When?~

~If, then.~ She nodded. ~Or if you are able to contact the deep earth—speak to it for me. It no long hears my voice.~ Her eyes closed tight, whole body brightening briefly.

~Reach the deep earth. That I might manage.~ He praised the breeze for its generosity and clarity in exchanging their words. ~And say what?~

~Thank it for me, but tell it I no longer need the sanctuary it offered. It is time to let go.~ She bent close, one hand hovering over his mouth. ~Do we have an agreement? ~

~Yes.~

An instant before he fell asleep, he saw her in full color, as she might have been in life: a brown-haired, brown-eyed woman with a haunted expression and the flickering remnants of bruises along the sides of her face and neck.

When he woke the next morning, two small chunks of cream-colored wax rested within the cup of his hand. Just the right size to tuck into his ears at the first opportunity. They might even go unnoticed for a while.

With them came the weight of expectations: that he would escape for himself, but also for her.

PART FOUR
LUELLA TOBIE

CHAPTER 15

SOMETHING UNSPECIFIED

Luella's first ride in an autowagon did not turn her into a fan. Her knuckles turned light, she held on so tight to the metal frame for fear of being bounced off. The wagon might not go as fast as a train, but proved far bumpier and jerkier. The driver took the narrow road—little more than a set of uneven ruts—at a much faster clip than Luella would dare, and she wished he didn't keep assuring her he knew the road as well as the back of his hand.

The seat had ample cushioning under the sleek brown upholstery, plus Luella wore the thickest, warmest suit of her three, and the honey wool skirt-pants added a little more protection between her and the jouncing springs. Alas, the suit didn't wash as easily as it should with the result that every time she bumped around, she wound up staring at a ship-shaped stain on one knee, as well as the tiny stitches along the cuffs and hems where May had mended it several times over. Whenever the road smoothed, or the driver slowed, she risked releasing a hand long enough to pat her hair and check the pins still held her heavy locks steady. She'd tucked her bead necklace down her shirt to reduce the havoc it wrought slinging this way and that around her neck.

May's many necklaces clacked away, though she'd pulled the collar of her suit jacket over them to keep them mostly in place. The rattle was almost-but-not-quite inaudible beneath the clang of the tires and the dings and bangs as the parts of the autowagon clashed. All that topped with a high-pitched whistle from the water spirit whirring in the engine whenever the wagon took a rise fast enough that all wheels left the ground. She, too, wore her warmest suit, but the blue unfortunately made it hard to miss the greenish cast around her mouth. Poor May had eaten a solid breakfast that morning while Luella, nervous or irritated or both at the continued lack of detail about the new job, had only drunk a little tea.

The driver was the same man who'd interviewed them back in Albany—Luella couldn't mistake the long-legged body or his face with a snub nose, merry green-brown eyes, and an impressive sprinkling of reddish freckles on otherwise light yellow-brown skin. He'd started the drive in a suit, but asked permission to doff his coat earlier. His white shirt sleeves flapped in the breeze, as did the three feathers stretching high above the others in his hat.

He grinned as he whirled the steering wheel this way and that. Yet whenever he smiled at Luella and May in the backseat, he seemed to take the next bump a little faster.

Even before the drive, Luella hadn't been sure he was really interested in having her take the job to find the item in question, but was unclear whether he doubted her worth or the value of searching for . . . whatever.

It didn't help that he kept telling them different things he was called—runner, summoner, long legs, my brother's keeper, my brother's extra legs—and whenever he shared another name his eyes twinkled, suggesting he joked with himself if not with them.

All in all, it didn't make for a good start to a new job even before the need to leave Albany arose. According to Runner, the only person who could satisfactorily describe the artifact Luella had agreed to locate wasn't in the city or planning to come back any time soon. At the initial meeting, Runner had given them many assurances that the item likely wasn't in the city either. He rolled his eyes as he spoke even though the older woman present to evaluate Luella and May gave him quite a look.

Luella didn't trust *him*, but respected the older woman. Darker of skin and with long gray hair kept in two braids, she'd worn a simple, old-fashioned round dress of deep blue and knitted away with clacking needles on something shapeless in red yarn. She'd asked few questions, all to the point, as she scrutinized the letters of recommendation May had provided. Alas, the older woman had decided to remain in the city. Perhaps she'd been a passenger when Runner drove an autowagon before.

Jun, too, was back in Albany.

Luella had had dinner with him the night before, with May, too, all of them in clean clothes and having had a wash. Jun took them to a Chinese restaurant, a fine place with red and gold decorations on pale gray walls, and round tables on which the servers placed a variety of meats and vegetables to be shared. He chose them with care, he explained, so that meats, vegetables, and sauces complemented each other and offered a variety. Luella enjoyed the eggplant and shrimp dish in particular—she could still almost taste it if she dared close her eyes.

"My uncle was brought here from Scranton," Jun said as

he showed Luella how to use chopsticks, May watching closely from around the table. "Evidently he'd started speaking with fire and this upset him to the point he stopped speaking at all."

"I thought you said he was an air speaker." Luella adjusted her hold on the smooth wooden sticks, laying them down and picking them up until over and over as they waited for food.

"He was—is." Jun grimaced as he corrected himself. "And he speaks to earth, too. Deyo Senior said he was possibly the oldest speaker with a high level of power that anyone at the Institute has seen. They think he might have done as well as he did because he balanced speaking to air and earth, until fire unbalanced him."

"What does he speak with now?" May asked.

"Air only, or so Deyo Senior thinks. Somehow, when he arrived at the Institute no one noted contact information for my grandparents or mother or anyone else in the family, or else it went missing." Jun's eyes narrowed as he passed the rice around. "Deyo Senior assured me that if they'd known he had family who valued him, they would have written to us to ask how we wished him cared for."

"You believe that?" May asked.

"I believe Cornelius Deyo was sincere, and his son as well, but not all of the scientists there would I trust far." Jun served himself last, adorning his plate with modest portions of rice, meat, and vegetables. "I was given all of my uncle's clothes and belongings, of that I'm sure."

A troubled expression crossed his face.

"You got everything you'd expect?" Luella picked up chopsticks and gingerly dug into the rice and eggplant.

A pensive expression crossing his face, then he nodded. "Yes. Even things that might bring good money if sold. The coin, of course, but also my uncle had a few books with him, and a bell, and several changes of clothing. He might have had more, but ... everything they kept at the Institute was something my uncle doesn't have with him. It makes no sense to take a man from all that is familiar, even his clothes, and send him somewhere else."

"That may make it all the more special when he sees that you have come for him." May smiled at Jun, only to have it fade. "If he recognizes you."

"He will." Jun lifted his chin. "My grandparents always used to say I looked much as my uncle did when he was young. I sent a telegram to my mother to report we found the coin and that I'm close to seeing uncle, and I'll send a longer letter first thing tomorrow. Speaking of which." He pulled a much-folded letter of recommendation from his pocket and handed it discreetly to May as he glanced back and forth between her and Luella. "Are you . . . staying in Albany or . . ."

Luella tried to respond, but no words came to mind.

After a brief silence, May stepped in. "We may have a job that will take us out of town a bit, but I think I speak for both of us when I say that we're interested in learning how things go, and hope that you can take your uncle home to your family."

Luella nodded, licking her lips and managing a smile.

Jun had shown pleasure at the news.

A particularly hard bounce broke Luella's reverie and brought her back to the present at an awful moment. The autowagon headed downhill at a fast clip. Her backside and hands ached from the ride, but the end was finally in sight: a village by the side of a long, thin lake. Storm clouds loomed in the distance, but enough light pierced the clouds that the buildings cast distinct shadows.

The town had only a few wide streets, and some narrower alleys. The buildings were a mix of styles, some similar to houses they'd passed going out of Albany—two or three stories with pitched roofs—and others such as Luella had never seen before.

Runner stopped the autowagon in front of a large inn where he promised to reserve a room for May and Luella, but allowed them only enough time to wash their faces before whisking them off to speak with the leaders. That required a short walk down three blocks to a log house with a fine view of the village and shore.

The house seemed small from the outside, but inside proved to be a single large room. The hearth sat at the center, with a raised metal basin laid with logs but unlit. A metal pipe in the ceiling directly above seemed to narrow to draw the smoke, but no doubt there were air speakers capable of asking breezes to carry the smoke up and out while leaving the heat behind.

Platforms ran the width of the sides of the house, supporting five finely carved wooden chairs and a table on which lay a long pipe. Backless benches lined the sides and the front, two deep, with a single long bench behind the five chairs.

There was no one there, but a door in a back corner sat slightly ajar, letting in a breeze so thick with moisture it was hard to breathe. Even the short walk from the inn had left Luella panting and with a light layer of sweat under her clothes.

"A few of the local chiefs and clan mothers will be here shortly," Runner said. "They will speak English, unless you understand Kanien'kéha?"

"Or they Mikasuki?" May raised her eyebrows.

Runner nodded, tapping his chest at the matching jibe.

"If they approve, and they likely will, then they'll take you, well, more likely they'll tell me to take you, to my brother who started this whole fool's quest, though don't call him fool or quester."

"*We* wouldn't." May shook her head.

"No, I would guess not." Runner grinned.

"What should we call him?" Luella asked, glancing around and catching a flash of gray through the crack in the far door.

"I'll have to think about that one." He'd donned his jacket after leaving the autowagon, but now took off his hat and turned it around and around on his hand. "It must be accurate, and polite, but also suitable for the occasion."

"Or perhaps you could tell us his name while you think of another?" May asked.

"He has such a sunshiny disposition that everything rolls off him." Runner shrugged. "Sometimes we call him Summer."

Luella made a note of the name, and promptly set it aside as the door on the far side opened wide and four people entered in an uneven line.

First was an older man still tall and straight but with a shock of white hair above a wrinkled face. His suit of fine gray hung about him slightly, as though made for a broader man. A much younger man followed close behind, in a darker gray, and gave him a subtle lift on the elbow as they clambered onto the platform. The two women following seemed between them in age, each with ample streaks of gray in their dark hair. One wore a round dress, and the other a suit similar to May and Luella's. The last had a distant resemblance to Runner, with a similar array of freckles on slightly darker skin, and the same nose but brown eyes. She gave him a level look, but the corners of her lips twitched in a small smile.

May handled most of the talking, stepping aside when Luella wanted to answer, but the whole was settled quick enough. Runner had it right—they approved her hire, and asked him to take her to his brother. It was just her and Runner, for the chiefs and clan mothers had asked May to stay and chat.

They went down from the longhouse to a rocky promontory overlooking a long narrow beach. Very narrow, with little more than a spit of cleared earth between the banks and the waves lapping higher every few tries.

The sun shone here, enough that the warm clothes Luella appreciated while bucketing along in the autowagon proved less of a blessing. The sunlight also fell on the far side of the lake, where a variety of small buildings clustered around a large one.

Yet the lake itself was mostly clouded over with dark gray that made the turgid waters seem deeper and unwelcoming.

At first, she wondered if Runner was trying to sneak up on his brother, he walked so quietly along the stepping stones that made a path between high, waving grasses. Luella made little noise, but her beads rolled this way and that across her chest, and the legs of her skirt-pants rustled in the damp air. Runner stopped on the stretch of stones and little growth, a few steps behind and to the side of Summer, who was frowning at the waves.

Summer did not seem sunshiny or summery at all, his face set in stern lines. Runner's brother was younger than she'd expected, although the older of the two. His skin was a deeper brown, with squint lines at the edges of his brown eyes, and hair short and full black. Summer had no freckles, and a longer face and features than Runner, but they had similar builds and loose-limbed movements, and appeared to patronize the same tailor.

"The beach is almost gone," Runner said.

"It may rain on the Hall, but the storms are dropping more and more water here." Summer didn't turn, just waved at the lake.

"How fast is it rising?" Runner asked.

"At this rate, we'll lose the last of the beach in a week or less, and the water will soon lap at some doorways." Summer turned and smiled at Luella—the shift completely changing his face into one that deserved being called sunshiny—and then cast a pointed glance at Runner.

"May I introduce . . ." Runner's eyes were narrowed and still focused on the lake, his brow furrowed. "My brother whom some call Summer. Brother, this is Luella Tobie, a finder with many recommendations for her ability to track lost things."

"I'm glad to meet you, and gladder still that you're good at finding things." Summer bowed to Luella.

"And I'm glad to meet you," Luella said. "Not least because no one yet has described exactly what it is I'm supposed to find, and they keep saying that you know."

"There's a good reason no one has described it." Summer grimaced, and Luella's right foot suddenly started to twitch. "Because we don't know exactly what it is."

"Or even if it exists," Runner added in a low voice nevertheless clearly meant to be heard by Summer and Luella both.

"Something of a certain nature must exist." Summer glanced at his brother but otherwise focused on Luella. "We need your help finding whatever bound that land,"—he pointed across the lake at the buildings—"to an English family centuries ago in such a way that the earth resists undoing the binding despite the way the magic twists the weather."

Luella swallowed hard. When they asked for someone to find something unspecified, they'd meant that? "Do you know anything about it? Size? Shape?"

Summer shook his head and turned out his hands.

"Nope," Runner added, rolling his eyes.

CHAPTER 16

FINDING THE UNKNOWN

Summer wanted Luella to find something he couldn't describe or swear existed?

Luella froze, before one face full of hope despite an aura of concern that hung about him, and the other doubtful.

A flicker of light drew her attention beyond them, to the storm hovering over the lake. Thunder rumbled, and waves rose high on the lake surface as rain pelted down, yet the storm didn't seem to move. Beyond, only pale gray clouds passed over the village or house or whatever lay on the green hillside. Light-colored bodies in bright attire walked along the beach and ventured into the water—was it not raining there?

There was something odd going on, certainly, but it wasn't any of her business. As for what was her work, she'd been brought out of the city by a denier to do the impossible.

"I find lost things. Rings, coins, packages, money, clothes, or . . . where people know what is missing, they just don't know where it is." Luella turned back to the brothers. "You give me a mystery instead.

"There are tales of seekers who work wonders." Summer smiled with a world of hope although his gaze was dark and intent on her.

"I prefer to call myself a finder," Luella said, though a spark of energy trickled down her spine at the word seeker.

"Tales of finders who work wonders, then." Summer nodded, smile dropping away but gaze unchanged. "Not long ago, during the Troubles, Rosa Tangeman walked these lands. She could tell a person's character by the way they stood on the earth, and find a person fitting a description, as long as it was particular enough and the person was within a certain radius. It's said she also knew what happened to those she loved no matter how far away. Or what about Rosa's uncle Jonny Tangeman, who could find any place on the continent, and guided the three who gave themselves to the deep earth."

A shiver ran down Luella's spine at the reference to *Them*. She glanced to either side, relieved when the area around remained free of people formed of ivy or other plant matter, or eyes of fire or teeth of stone.

Despite winds blowing across the lake, the storm seemed to grow backward and a fine mist began to fill the air. Droplets formed along Luella's arms and clung to her nose and eyelashes.

"I'm no Rosa or Jonny Tangeman." By all accounts the pathwalkers of fame and glory had immense powers. Luella's smaller gift-curse had brought her quite enough trouble as-was, and she didn't need or want to stride across the land working marvels.

"You don't need to be, but it gives me hope that you find *things*." Summer brushed moisture from his forehead, then brought out an umbrella from behind a rock. Big and unwieldy, it had a long wooden handle and spokes holding up bright orange rain-proofed canvas. It stretched wide enough to shelter all three, if they huddled close.

At least the warmth of the two men's bodies helped balance the growing rain-chill in the air.

"I find things that are lost, that are known to be lost." Luella hoped the repetition would get it into his head.

"You did find that lost coin across three, four states and hundreds of miles." Runner stood behind her, chest brushing her arm as he breathed.

"Things that people can describe to me or show me a picture. A drawing or photo." She turned her head to glare back at him. "I thought you doubted this . . . whatever . . . exists."

"I doubt." Runner's smile did not resemble his brother's, holding far too much devilment. "But I also believe in my brother, and *he* believes."

"*He* can speak for himself," Summer said from his place next to Luella, positioned to keep watch over both the lake and distant shore. "Still, that's a truth. I believe. The fact that you're here, close to the Hall should help. You don't have to reach across vast distances."

"Assuming this thing does exist, are you sure it's still there?" Luella waved at the far side of the lake.

"Yes," Summer said.

Luella waited, but he offered no additional information. "And?"

"Good question." Laughter filled Runner's words.

"Whose side are you on?" Summer chuckled as he threw a rueful glance at his brother.

Runner made no answer, but stretched out his arms to

either side, rain slicking his hands as they extended beyond the umbrella.

"Ignore him." Summer shook his head, shifting to face Luella although he had to look down to do so, and she up. "I am a binder, one of a number in the nation."

"One of the strongest," Runner said.

A hint of red darkened Summer's cheeks, but he continued. "My fellows and I have spent hours, days, undoing the tangle of bindings that keeps that land solid and causes it to behave so oddly. The earth protects the buildings and people to an extreme degree that we've never seen or heard of anywhere else, warping the weather to the point storms never strike there, only gentle rain and breezes, as you can see."

And feel, as the rain intensified over this shore, although the wind kept blowing east.

"In winter, snow falls but never too much," Summer continued, "and more falls elsewhere to compensate. Lightning never strikes there, though now it yearns to."

With perfect timing, lighting arced toward the largest house on the far shore. The bolt bent backward and struck the lake instead. A gout of steam rose alongside the rumble of thunder.

"You unbound the earth, but it's still . . ." Luella shivered.

"We found countless coercive bindings." Summer touched his fingers many times; a dozen, two. Remembered counting of the bindings? He swayed. "Those are the easiest to break, for one side often longs to be free. There were also other bindings—beneficial but oddly set and mingled with the coercive—still we worked to undo them to take the land back to itself alone to decide what it wished."

"It took ages. He and the others were worn out after

their last long session." Runner gripped his brother's shoulder, steadying the older man.

"Despite all our work, the underlying binding, the first, remains. We have undone it a half-dozen times, yet even as we untangle the threads, the earth restores them and rebinds itself. A cousin who speaks with earth spirits came to help, but said the earth there does not listen—cannot seem to even hear her. She fears it is caught, trapped, unable to understand how the binding is tainting all around. Yet that binding was first made centuries ago. Whichever humans bargained for it are long dead, for it was set shortly after the English first arrived here in numbers. We think they used a token to represent the binding. A sword, perhaps, or a scroll or . . . whatever it is, I am convinced it must still be there." He pointed, drawing a circle around the buildings and land. "If it were elsewhere, distance and lack of knowledge would contribute to the bond's decay, but it remains strong."

"I'm not a binder, and I don't know enough of what you do." Luella knew—who could not?—that binders and worked stone and metal gave parts of the world stability for humans.

Seminole binders cherished and nurtured agreements with the lands where she'd grown up, allowing plants to move about while ensuring crops remained in selected places. Tending the villages and deciding when and where to build houses and structures that would last only a few seasons or years, and where they might raise longer-term settlements.

It was one thing to know they worked their magic, and another to understand the how.

"I'm willing to believe there's something there, as you do, but that doesn't mean I can find it." Cold doubts warred with wishes, chilling her insides. Perhaps her power wasn't that strong, but what if it were? Could she manage it, and send word of the accomplishment to the Little Bird clan mothers who'd sent her away?

Or would trying push her too far?

"There is no guarantee of success, but will you try?" Summer asked.

"We don't know what it is!" The rain slowed and lightened as the storm split and went around the place across the lake. Luella stepped out from under the umbrella, cooler without the closeness to the two men.

"Have you never found anything without knowing it?" Summer let the umbrella fall to Runner to disassemble. He crossed his arms over his chest, head tilted to one side as he studied her.

No hovered on Luella's tongue, but she swallowed it as a pair of breezes flicked around her, one warm and one cool.

When small, she'd played games of hot and cold, finding things she wanted but didn't have words for—food, parents, pets—by turning her body this way and that, moving away from cold and toward warmth.

"Maybe."

"Let me tell you about the Hall and its early history." Summer waved at a number of large boulders clustered near a tall maple. Several had flat sections suitable for use as seats. No doubt binders had worked with the rocks, encouraging them to adjust or to allow human alteration for just that purpose. "Perhaps that will help you find what we seek."

"I'll go get food and drink, for you'll need that if you keep talking." Runner set the umbrella back into a depression in the earth next to the rocks, then headed off.

Luella's backside still ached from the bouncing of the

autowagon. Instead of taking a seat, she leaned against the tree. The trunk was warm against her back. With the storm moving around, the sun had come out overhead and heated the humid air. She undid the top buttons of her blouse and ran a handkerchief along her forehead and throat.

"So?" She shifted her stance against the tree so that she could see both Summer and the buildings across the way, or the main hall at least.

"They came here nearly three hundred years ago." Summer settled on a nearby boulder. "They were not the first Europeans, or the first English. Albany was settled several decades earlier, as a fort before a town, but these people,"—he nodded at the hall—"came as a family. Father, mother, several grown children with their spouses and younglings, and a number of servants."

That explained the extent of the land and buildings, though surely it took time and much negotiation to raise so many and such a big house at the center.

"Our stories say we did not know they were there until after they had begun to build and bargain with the land." He grimaced, a hiss slipping through clenched teeth. "That they somehow chose the perfect spot to escape our notice, a place we claimed and tended some of the time, and other times was held by the Mohican. However they chose the place, they had time to settle and build before we came across them."

"And once they were there, they were harder to remove?" She'd grown up on plenty of similar stories.

Summer nodded. "Our chiefs bargained with them rather than trying to push them out, because the English already had the deep earth's favor, and the tangle of bindings grew from there."

"Is there anything else you know that would help?"

Nothing in his account gave her any sense of what she should look for, despite the faint prickling sensation along her spine.

"Their leader was fleeing for his life from England. He had done something for which he was certain they would hunt him down, or so we are told, and when he came here his family called the place their sanctuary."

"*What?*" An unusual word that she hadn't heard often, which made the prickling increase.

"Sanctuary Hall. It's owned by the Whistle family, since they first built."

"As in the Whistle Institute in Albany?" Luella stepped away from the tree and shaded her eyes so as to get a better look. Jun's uncle might be in one of the buildings.

A feeling of warmth rippled through her, as though a flame licked up along the side facing the Institute—completely obliterating the prickle.

Was she sensing the presence of Jun's uncle, thanks to proximity, or whatever Summer sought?

Or neither?

CHAPTER 17
FAILING AT FINDING

Luella curled up at the foot of the tree she'd leaned against several days earlier. A break in the clouds overhead allowed afternoon sun to beat down on her dark blue linen shirt and skirt-pants, as the area finally reached a temperature she considered warm if not hot. Her aching muscles rejoiced in the sun, loosening and leaving her a subdued heap resting atop roots and grasses. Her hair hung in long braids swinging against her back. Breezes twirled around, but out over the lake another storm grew.

Wisps of gray clouds whirled, whipping the surface of the lake into a frothy confection of waves. The few boats that had sailed out earlier in the day all returned to shore—leaving the waters to the storm. Once again, people in bright swimming outfits frolicked on the beach across the way. No one did so on this side. The beach was nearly gone, the rising waters swallowing it bit by bit.

How many storms since Luella arrived in the village? At least one each day, but she'd lost count.

Weary to the bone, she rested unwilling—unable—to

sense things around her excepting only those that lived and breathed and moved.

The tree, whose roots outlined a comfortable curved space for her to curl up within while its branches reached down to brush her, leaving scattered green leaves atop her body.

The grasses, gathered together to provide a soft space to lay her head in full understanding their blades would bend or break.

The breezes, splintered off from the storm winds to carry whispers and words of encouragement and concern to her ears. Voices she recognized—Runner, a chief or clan mother or two, faithkeepers, the people working at the inn, and the area binders most notably Summer.

May.

Regular thuds along the stone path warned her of an approach, an intrusion, but she lacked the energy to move. Even tracking the footsteps took energy. The rustle of skirt-pants suggested a woman's approach, mixed with the clack of beads. Luella guessed at May's arrival even before the older woman settled on a nearby boulder.

"There's no shame in not succeeding. You tried, over and over."

Kind words, but they hurt all the same.

Luella didn't move her head or make any acknowledgment that she'd heard. Two vistas lay before her: one that she saw with her eyes and another with her mind. If she wanted, she could rise and walk into either—, but she'd have to take care where she put her feet.

Moving in the physical world, the true vista, would lead her into the lake or back to the village.

The other view offered the chance to cross a line in the earth with a slippery slope on the other side. It wasn't a now-or-never opportunity, as Vic had described it, but rather a choice of which she was increasingly aware. Made aware. Unable to refuse to be aware that she could, at any time she wanted, step onto the path.

She'd still be a finder, but she'd no longer *not* be a path-walker. She'd change, be changed.

She wasn't willing to give up the possibility of going home to stay.

"You did try." This time, May's voice started as a sentence and swung upward, not quite turning it into a question.

"I tried playing hot and cold, and following what little heat I could find here—and went in circles. I tried closing my eyes and turning around and around until I didn't know which direction was what, which took a long time because I know where my belongings are in the inn better than I'd thought, but I managed it in the end and went in that direction and nearly fell into the lake." Luella shivered at memory of the close call before a tree root had lashed around her ankles and pulled her back.

"That's a start."

"Summer and two sailors took me out on the lake time after time, day and night, going as close to the shore as we could without attracting notice. We fished, and caught lots of fish, most of which we threw back, but I didn't sense anything of value on the shore." Luella nestled her head more firmly on the grass. "I asked if we could get out, but Summer said the Kanien'kehá:ka were banned from setting foot on the land there, and since I was in the canoe with them they didn't want to take the chance the ban included me. Apparently the earth there either doesn't let us leave the water or on the first footstep out throws us back in."

"I didn't think things would be this complicated." May

sighed. Grass rustled as she crossed and settled near Luella, stroking her braids. "Are you sorry you came?"

Yes. No. Both.

More thuds and rustles as some of the binders came over to perch on the boulders. Summer, unmistakable in his usual gray. A woman about May's age, though shorter and stouter, in a long dark-orange dress who always smelled a little of pipe smoke even though Luella had never seen her smoke or carry a pipe, and whom she'd been told she might call Smoke. A man introduced as a Deskahe, a chief and a binder in the form of an old, frail elder in dusty brown who leaned on a carved walking stick taller than he was.

Fitting that they had come, because Luella had some information to share, though she wasn't sure of how much value. She pushed up to sit sideways, legs still within the curve of the roots but back against the tree. Bits of grass trickled down from her hair and clothes as a kind breeze cleaned her of vegetation.

"I may have dreamed of it last night," Luella said.

"Of what?" May asked, but the others heard. They hadn't been talking anyway, but froze and made no noise whatsoever.

"It. The talisman for the Hall." Luella waved at the house across the lake.

A long pause, and out of the corner of her eye she caught May exchanging puzzled glances with the binders. The Deskahe and Smoke held some kind of conversation with their eyes, then nodded at May, who asked, "What is it?"

"I don't know." She fought the urge to snuggle back down into an O within the space the roots had opened for her.

"But you dreamed . . ."

"I dreamed a lot, not just about that." Luella frowned. "Or I don't think it was just that."

May nodded. "I heard you screaming."

"Did I?" Luella tracked the expansion of the storm, clouds grown to twice their previous size but not yet dropping rain on the swollen lake. "I'm sorry if I woke anyone."

"I took your hand and cradled you, and you fell back into sleep." May ran a hand along Luella's arm. "What did you dream?"

Luella stretched and pulled to her feet, holding onto the tree as she turned to face May and the binders.

"There were two dreams or three or four, I'm not sure of the number. The first or all but the last involved running. It was dark night, no moon but no clouds or rain either. I had a long gown on, very loose, and nothing else, and I ran across a field of mown grass until a great wind swept down and carried me off, lifting me high as though I had wings. That was glorious." She pulled her shoulders back, for a moment reliving the sensation of being weightless and buoyed by warm winds. "Then something"—someone— "on the ground looped ivy around my ankle and pulled me back down."

"Then I was back at the beginning, running across grass down toward the lake." Luella pointed at the waves below, then shrugged and turned her hand out, "a lake or big body of water. An immense wave rushed up on the shore to grab me and lift me almost as high before. But again, something looped ivy around my ankle and yanked me from the water."

It might not have been the woman of ivy she'd seen before—she could hope. What would one of *Them* be doing in her dreams anyway?

"Was that all?" May whispered, eyes and mouth open wide.

"Last, I ran through trees and along a hillside. Up then down or the reverse. I wore more clothes this time, layers of heavy skirts that I had to twist my hands in to hold them above my ankles. Tight shoes that pinched my toes. A bodice that cinched and flattened me. My face hurt all along one side." Luella stroked her right cheek. It felt whole to the touch but brought back memories of blood or something smelling of copper trickling down from her temple. "There were bruises along my arms and legs, and my back. I tripped but fell into soft earth. Mud? Or not, but the earth held me, cradled me, kept me safe.

"Gave me . . . sanctuary, and a meeting of spirits." That was warmth and heat and comfort beyond anything she'd known since she was small enough to be cradled in her parents' arms.

Luella shivered, jerking away from the tree and nearly stumbling forward. "Then the earth swallowed me whole. I couldn't breathe until it spat me into a small stone room with no windows, no doors, no nothing. And it stank. A sweetly awful smell that got into my nose and wouldn't leave. Skeletal fingers appeared before me, bone white against the darkness. Two sets. One pair held something glowing green. The other turned a sour yellow color and reached for me as though to pluck out my eyes.

"That's when I woke. Maybe when I screamed."

"Dreams into a nightmare." May stroked Luella's back. Luella leaned into her and her warmth, even if it was less than memory of the earth in the dream.

"Air, water, and earth." Smoke rested her chin on a hand, fingers rapping against her thigh.

"No fire?" Summer asked.

"Fire is waiting." Luella slapped her hands over her mouth, not sure where the words came from.

With perfect timing, lightning blazed across the lake and thunder boomed. The agitated waves caught bits of light back in a partial reflection. The storm cracked open to let rain fall onto the lake without ever touching the lands around the Hall. None of the rain fell on the near side, yet, but the humidity in the air increased.

"No wonder you screamed," May said.

"The faithkeepers may have some wisdom to add, if you are willing to share your dreams with them or allow us to do." The Deskahe shook his head. "I don't like the notion of fire waiting."

"That's all right, but . . ." Movement in the distance caught Luella's eye. She froze for a moment, fearful that she'd see a woman or man made of ivy. If there was, they vanished the instant she turned.

She teetered, as though standing atop a hill trying not to fall—not to slide over a line scratched in the earth. Then a voice in the distance called her name, and May's, and the sensation subsided.

"Jun?" May asked, peering around Luella.

Feet thudded against stone. The sound threatened to bring back memories of the dream again, until Jun raced down the hill and arrived huffing before her. His clothes were slightly awry and his hair wind-blown. Two suited men from the Institute—the two Deyos—followed in the distance, looking quite uncomfortable. Runner walked alongside them, eyebrows high.

"Help me find my uncle," Jun panted.

"But they—isn't he being brought from there?" Luella pointed through the storm at the Hall.

"They sent word there's some kind of a problem, and

then nothing. No letters, no telegrams." Jun thrust his fingers through his hair, leaving thick runnels. "We can't even get to the Hall, because the river is up over the bridge. Something's wrong. Can you at least tell me if he's there or somewhere?"

Luella wanted to say she didn't find people, but Jun knew that and asked her anyway.

"I'll try." She turned to May. "Don't let me stumble far from where I am, all right?"

Without waiting for May's nod, Luella closed her eyes. Turned around and around, focusing on Jun and his love for his uncle. The photo she'd seen at the start, and Jun's drawing, floated through her mind's eye. She felt tugged in two directions. Stopping in place, she lifted her arms and pointed.

One finger nearly touched Jun's forehead.

The other aimed directly at the Hall.

"So he's there." Jun closed his eyes and murmured something in Chinese.

"Missing, or in hiding, or my cousin is lying to us." Cornelius Deyo's face turned whiter than Luella would have thought possible. "And my daughter is there!"

"On the other side of the storm," Summer said, "where we cannot go."

CHAPTER 18

STORMS OUTSIDE AND INSIDE

Once again Luella huddled against wood, but this time she retreated into a far corner of the log cabin. A crowd lined the room, filling it with warmth. The scents of sweat and recent meals mingled into an overall general musk. Some sat on benches, others stood in place or moved around. Most of the conversation was in English, but small groups farther from the platform—and hence closer to Luella—regularly broke into discussions in the local language that made it harder for her to hear the chiefs, sub-chiefs, clan mothers, and faithkeepers crowded on the platform.

Or the Kanien'kehá:ka binders, Jun, and Cornelius Deyo facing them. May stood nearby, but off to one side. Runner was at a far corner of the platform, kneeling or sitting lower than the chiefs. The younger Deyo had started behind his father, but slowly been pushed back, or let himself be pushed back, into the corner opposite Luella.

Her stomach rumbled, but she took little note. Time enough for food later.

Only May and Jun paid any attention to Luella, and even that was little more than a glance now and then.

Luella didn't belong here. She hadn't found the item they hired her to find—she was increasingly certain it would require stepping on the path, although even then there was no certainty. Vic hadn't promised she'd have any more power than she did now if she went on the path, just that if she didn't, she'd dwindle.

Which still didn't sound too bad. She could go home, then, promise not to find things that weren't any of her business, and work in the fields.

Or was it too late?

A flash of green had her stiffening, arms pinned close against her sides as she looked around for a person made of ivy.

Three passes turned up no one. Only then did she relax.

A hard edge in the older Deyo's voice caught her attention. She missed what he said, but one of the chiefs—the binder the Deskahe complete with his walking stick to lean on—rose and pointed at the roof.

Rain drummed, interspersed with occasional rumbles of thunder, but the chief's voice carried across the sounds of nature and the hubbub of English and Kanien'kéha.

"You have seen the storms looming around Sanctuary Hall, and how the waters of the lake have risen." He tilted his walking stick in the direction of the lake.

"Yes." Deyo nodded, swaying slightly.

"We sent to you, asking for help to redress this." The Deskahe leaned on the table. "You did nothing."

Deyo's head and shoulders slumped. His son left the far corner and began squeezing through the crowd to stand behind his father again.

They should be sorry. Luella hadn't produced anything,

but she'd at least tried.

"Now you come to ask us for help. What do you offer in balance?" The chief sat back, hands folded in his lap.

"I don't know yet. Let me think what is fitting." Deyo rubbed his temples and lifted his head. "How long has the weather been out of balance?"

"The extent was documented six years ago, but we believe it has been longer. It took time to grow to the point we were certain." A woman sitting next to the chief spoke. She looked to be May's age or younger, with long brown hair in braids and a resonant voice that carried easily.

"It may be due to the concentration of speakers housed at the Hall, all unable to communicate with humans, but in constant discussion with air and water." Deyo turned out his hands. "I will see about ways to disperse them more widely."

"That is acceptable, but alone not enough," the chief said.

Near Deyo, Jun vibrated with intensity. "What do we do now? My uncle is there."

Before the Deskahe or any of the other leaders could respond, someone drummed at the door. The person closest, a man of middling age, opened it slightly, started, and cast a puzzled look or request for help to the platform. He said something, but not in English.

Runner slipped through the crowd with speed and ease, reaching the door and conducting a quick, low-voiced conversation with whomever stood on the other side. Whipping back to the platform, he whispered something to the gathered leaders.

The Deskahe waved a hand. "Let him in."

The door opened wide, allowing Vic to stride in—or, rather, squelch. He was soaked head to toe, every inch of his muddy shirt and pants sticking to his body, but he held out a hand holding a metal badge before him. The crowds drew back, some of the standers squishing onto the benches.

"Victor Stanton Jones, pathwalker and agent of the Federal Bureau of Magical Investigation," Vic bowed to the royá:ner, sparing a quick glance around and a brief nod at Luella. "Under the authority of the President, as delegated by the Reconstituted Congress in which the Kanien'kehá:ka have due representation and local territorial authority, I have come to offer aid and counsel, and request the same in return."

A rustle of interest rippled around the room. Or suspicion? Luella couldn't tell. He sounded strong, but winded, yet managed to rattle off the sentence with a practiced air. On the far side, Summer and Smoke sat tall and watched the new arrival with keen eyes.

"We welcome you and will hear your counsel and discuss aid and return, but we have business before us." The Deskahe gestured at the Deyos and Jun.

"So I've heard in the village. I believe I can speak to that matter for it overlaps with mine."

"Speak on, then, but be brief," the Deskahe said.

The older Deyo opened his mouth, but shut it without saying anything.

"You've gathered because the bridge to Sanctuary Hall is out of commission and storms threaten the village with rising water—though they leave the Hall alone?" Vic asked.

"Yes, but the storms and high water are the result of years of the weather being out of balance." The chief sat back crossing his arms over his chest. "Due, we believe, to Sanctuary Hall's bindings having become twisted."

"There's more twisted than that." Vic grimaced, turning again to glance around. "Over the years, the Bureau has had an increase in complaints about captive spirits powering autowagons. Nothing much to go on at first, as the spirits when freed promptly rejoin their element and offer no testimony whatsoever, even when we have willing speakers at the ready. We've had little more than a chain of whispers pointing to the source being somewhere in northern New York."

Jun started forward, but May grabbed his arm and whispered in his ear. The older Deyo turned as pale as he had before, and his son clapped his hand over his mouth, eyes wide. In contrast, the Kanien'kehá:ka largely settled into silence with many heads nodding and lips pressed tight, as though this was unfortunate but not unexpected.

"Near here, I take it." The Deskahe tilted his head toward the lake and the Hall opposite.

"Indeed." Vic nodded. "I'm a pathwalker specializing in places. The case was handed to me recently with a request to find where the spirits are being captured. My path led me initially to the Whistle Institute. It's become clear no one there is *actively* involved, but that is not true of Sanctuary Hall."

The news did not ease the Deyos, or Jun. Luella rose and walked as quiet as she could through the narrow aisles down to join May and Jun near the front. Jun grabbed her hand when she pressed next to him, fingers clenching hard.

"That would explain the imbalance in the weather." The clan mother clicked her tongue.

"Yes, even more than the concentration of speakers in their last days," another woman on the bench behind the chiefs offered. "If the captive spirits are air and water, the elements would be angered to the point of storms."

"But the problem remains that the earth is protecting the Hall," a young man siting next to her added.

"And George Whistle has forbidden us to set foot on the land, unless invited, in such a manner that the earth keeps us away." The Deskahe frowned.

"I can make an official request for access—" Vic started, but the older Deyo interrupted.

"I can do more than that." He stood straight, pale and sweating and obviously wrought up, but waited for the chief to acknowledge him before continuing. "Sanctuary Hall does not belong to my cousin, George Whistle. He bought it at auction but could not afford to keep and repair it. So the Institute purchased it from him and leases it to him as long as he cares for speakers, for which he receives funds from us and the State. You asked earlier what I can offer you in balance and redress. I hereby grant you and your nation the right to pass over the land at will."

Low whispers and nods mixed with raised chins and dubious glances.

Jun vibrated next to Luella, but kept silent. She swayed, Deyo Senior's intensity and willingness to give up what he'd held struck her as though . . . someone had wrapped ivy around her ankle and yanked her into the chamber.

"More, if it is proved that my cousin or anyone in authority at the Hall abused the speakers to imprison spirits for profit,"—Deyo drew in a deep breath—"then I will ensure the Institute reassigns ownership and returns it to the Kanien'kehá:ka."

The leadership stared at him for several breaths. They whispered together in their language, so even the few syllables Luella heard meant nothing to her. Vic likewise leaned over to whisper in Deyo's ear, something that caused his jaw to tighten.

At length, the Deskahe nodded. "The offer is accepted, and balance will be maintained."

"But how do we get there? My uncle is there." Jun pulled free from Luella and May to face the clan leadership and Vic and the Deyos. "He speaks with air, earth, and fire."

"Now that we have permission to go on the land, we can take boats to the shore." The Deskahe stood.

A long boom of thunder rolled through the room, setting Luella's teeth vibrating.

The Deskahe winced. "If the storm allows, or our air and water speakers can convince the elements to allow us passage."

Summer raised his head, speaking when acknowledged. "We still have to find whatever binds the earth to protect the Hall."

He stared at Vic, not Luella. A quick round of whispers swirled around the room.

The other pathwalker turned out his hands. "I can try, if it is a place you're looking for. But for things, I'm not so well suited." He shifted to face Luella, eyebrows lifting as he looked her over. His lips pursed, but he said nothing more.

Runner's mutter came through loud and clear in the sudden quiet. "We still don't know for certain there's an artifact."

Amid the rueful laughter and Summer's retort that it did exist, Luella's vision doubled. She stood in the room, and at the edge of a line on the far side of which lay a slippery slope to rolling hills up and down, down and up.

Everything would change, but Vic was right. A now or never point existed, and she'd reached it. She could stay safe on the one side and dwindle, or step up, step over, and be something more.

"I'll find it." She stood and took a long step toward the men in the center of the room.

Onto the path.

CHAPTER 19

STEPPING ON THE PATH

For the first time in a long time, Luella was warm through and through. Nothing hurt in the slightest. Darkness enfolded her, so complete that she could not see her hand before her face—if she were even able to hold it there.

Yet wherever she was wasn't comfortable. She lay on something firm, unable to move. The air was thick and heavy with a musty, sweet putrid odor that clung to the inside of her nose.

An all-too familiar smell that had infused her dream.

Thankfully, no skeletal hands reached for her.

But where was she? The path should have let her locate the artifact Summer and the other binders sought. It had brought her here instead. As herself? Or perhaps this was a waking dream.

Vic might have said something about being on the path providing more information, but Luella had not expected anything like this. Such dreams she could live without.

Little irony that she hadn't wanted to step on the path, and regretted having done it an instant later. But also not, for Jun deserved to find his uncle—hopefully still well whether or not able to speak with him. Summer had earned the binding talisman so he and the others could undo the earth's protection of the Hall, and it didn't hurt that in one go he'd thus prove his brother's faith in him and show his brother Summer was right.

Luella had thought to make that happen, but how could this turn into that?

Flickers of gray-silver luminescence danced in the darkness without illuminating anything. The pinpoints of light slowly circled and coalesced into a human form. A ghastly pale woman loomed over Luella. Blank eyes were set to either side of a long nose in an oval face. Her hair was pulled back tightly into a large chignon except for a few curls or strands that had escaped. Clothing manifested around her: an immense gown with wide skirts, long sleeves, and a flat bodice edged with fine lace.

Several necklaces circled her neck, almost hidden under the intricate patterned lace. A small cross hung from one just below her throat. Another was formed of beads, the ends falling under her bodice. She stroked the beads and chains, then pulled on one. A soft green light began to emerge from under the fabric.

Bit by bit, she withdrew a small stone, smooth but with a hole through the center where the chain passed. The stone glowed the light green of new shoots in the field springing up after winter. Waves of warmth rolled off it, bathing Luella with peace and security.

In an instant, the stone vanished. The woman remained, but reduced to faint silver lines against the dark. The warmth, peace, and security remained—pulsing over Luella's heart.

Tears trickled down the woman's cheeks. She spoke—

at least her mouth moved but she made no sounds and Luella couldn't guess what she said.

Though in that moment, the sound of Luella's name broke the silence.

May's voice, and Jun's, and Vic's, one at a time or all at once.

The darkness and woman dissolved—thankfully taking the horrendous odor with them. Luella woke with a start. Her eyes flew open, the roof overhead almost completely invisible behind the dozens of faces craning to look over her.

She lay on the floor, boards hard beneath her bottom and legs. Her head rested in May's lap. One of the clan mothers held her wrist, fingers pressing against Luella's pulse. Jun held Luella's other hand.

The heat dissipated with the vision, but she remained warm albeit dry mouthed. There was a circle of space around her and those closest, but many people remained in the chamber. She didn't have to see or hear them to know. Their presence impinged on her, if not so strongly as her awareness of things. If asked, she could pinpoint the exact location of the pipe on the table, even though she couldn't see it. Identify each of the Kanien'kehá:ka carrying weapons, the angle at which the Deskahe held his staff, and tell Vic exactly where he'd hidden several blades in his clothes.

The increased awareness of everything around her was too much. She didn't want to know exactly how many layers of clothes anyone wore, or how many pins kept up certain women's and men's hair, or how many feathers it took to make the Kanien'kehá:ka men's hats.

"It's too much. I can't . . ." She closed her eyes and pulled in her shoulders, hugging herself.

"Take it easy." Vic grasped her hand, his fingers rough and callused though no more so than most of the others in the room. "I know it's hard. Distracting. Pick something and focus on it. Let the rest fall way. Everything's the way it's always been. You know more about it now, but you don't have to know consciously. You'll get used to it. For now, let go."

Easier for him to say than her to do.

He wanted her to pick something to focus on. What else to choose but the item she'd been hired to find, the artifact she'd dreamed of, the stone circle resting across the lake.

Opening her eyes again, she looked for Summer in the crowd, knowing which way to glance after the notion crossed her mind. Runner stood next to him, arm along his shoulder.

"It does exist." Her voice cracked, but she forged on. "I know where it is, and I can lead you there."

CHAPTER 20

BINDING THE LAND

Luella crouched in first of several canoes heading across the lake. She perched on a thick cushion, but water sloshed around the bottom of the boat dampening her feet and splashing on the hem of the gray knit knee-length shorts she'd been loaned from the village holdings. Only the drawstring at the waist kept the shorts from falling off. The matching shirt of the two-piece swim suit had elbow-length sleeves and fell to mid-thigh. Her toes curled against the soft sandals that protected her soles but little more.

Despite the flimsy attire and cool of night, she was warm and had been ever since stepping on the path, a matter that displeased her the more she thought on it, so she'd set it aside to ponder later.

Nearly everyone else crossing the lake in the four canoes was similarly attired in village-provided swim suits, all two-piece outfits in soft, faded colors. Vic shared a canoe with Luella, and Jun and May another, while both Deyos sat in a third. Summer and Smoke traveled in the fourth, but they had their own swim attire, as did all the Kanien'ke-há:ka, and even they'd chosen subtle colors capable of blending into the dimness of the stormy lake. One sat at the front of each canoe and another at the rear, sending the boats gliding across the waters with swift, quiet strokes.

Only a faint hint of light attended their passage in the early hours of morning. Storm clouds thick with rumbling thunder blocked the moon while lightning regularly danced across the sky without touching land nearby. No canoe carried lamp or lantern, although the rims and oars were smeared with a waterproof substance that gave off a faint light blue luminescence. They left a mostly dark village behind, headed for an equally dark shore. One window in the great house before them gleamed with golden lamplight, but no more. Luella's eyes slowly adjusted to degrees of darkness, distinguishing between that which reflected light in some degree and that which did not.

The first canoe carried a water speaker and an air speaker, both Kanien'kehá:ka. They were Luella's age or even younger, chosen for their energy and power, though neither spoke more than a few words. It was easy to distinguish between them even several canoe-lengths behind. The water speaker bent low and trailed a hand along the rise-and-fall of the waves. The air speaker tilted their head back, and their long black hair danced in the wind. Watching, Luella stroked the still-neat braids controlling her hair —she didn't envy the air speaker the combing and brushing they'd need later.

Such power they had, yet she'd noticed the worry on the older Deyo's face after meeting them the evening before. The man stepped aside with the Deskahe, who stood near the cabin with his staff firmly planted on the earth. Their words, although soft, reached Luella perched on a nearby bench.

"The speakers are powerful, but this trip will do them no favors," Deyo said. "I've seen their like a hundred times or more. They have ten more years, perhaps fifteen if they are fortunate, before the elements take them."

Ten to fifteen more years, where Luella had stepped on the path but likely had many decades to go if Vic was any measure. Maybe even time enough to find a way to go home and stay. She counted her blessings.

"We know." The Deskahe leaned on his staff, tears glinting in his eyes. "We cherish them, and have hopes to keep them longer, but when the time comes we will let them go."

He and the other leaders let them go across the lake, and Luella, for one, was grateful for their presence. The waves calmed to allow the canoes swift, easy passage—even shifting to set up a current flowing exactly where they wanted to go. The storm winds blew from behind, pushing the boats along.

The paddlers wielded their oars regardless of assistance from air and water, to show they did not ask of the elements without also giving of their own labor.

The remnants of wrecked boats littered the lake bottom, some mostly intact and others down only to a few remaining spars or planks. Luella shivered every time the canoe passed over one. They were easier to ignore than her awareness of the travelers and what they carried: oars, knives, a bow and arrow, and food and drink wrapped in waterproof cloth.

Chilly, brackish water at the bottom of the canoe sloshed as Luella shifted on her cushion. She needed to move and generate heat. Only her chest was truly warm. A heavy weight rested there, a connection to the stone they sought pressing against her breastbone—and no necklace. She'd left her beads with the rest of her belongings, though she had two bead necklaces now. May had given Luella one of her own with a few words of praise.

That warmed her. Likewise the moment that Vic had shaken Luella's hand and said, "Well done. It would have taken me much longer to find the place where it rested." And gone on about possible employment and what the Bureau could offer her, talk cut short as the expedition came together.

A stray strand of rain damped her face, cool but not cold. She licked her lips and tasted a hint of smoke from the lightning, perhaps.

Luella had only taken the first step on the path. There would be more, but this was part of growing up. Her path wouldn't be the same as Vic's. Maybe she could find a way to shape it to linger near home as much as possible.

The first boat reached the far side of the lake. The lead paddler leaped out into thigh-deep water and started to pull the boat up onto the shore—only to stop where the water lapped against a narrow spit of sand edged with hard-packed earth and grass.

She leaned forward, straining, but was unable to step out of the water onto the sand.

"Bring me as near as you can to shore," the elder Deyo whispered, words twisting and almost echoing over the water. The third canoe carried him close. He nearly upset it as he lurched out, splashing and sending ripples every way. Luella gripped the edge of the canoe tight as waves rocked it.

Deyo waded onto the beach, easily leaving the water.

He crouched and laid both hands, one on grass and the other sand. "On behalf of the Whistle Institute that holds legal title to this land, I, Cornelius Deyo, descended from the Whistles who built Sanctuary Hall, give permission for all Kanien'kehá:ka, all Haudenosaunee, all people to walk upon it as they need."

Nothing happened for a moment. The canoes bobbed on slow, rolling waves, then the Kanien'kehá:ka woman ankle-deep in water walked ashore.

Within moments, all canoes were close enough in for everyone to make their way to the shore. The paddlers dragged the empty boats high onto land so that even rising waters were unlikely to loosen them soon. A few paddlers remained with the boats, and the rest formed a crowd around the passengers.

Luella shivered, although the air was warmer away from the water. Damp cloth stuck to her thighs and arms.

The air speaker smiled at her, then waved a hand. Gentle breezes twined around her and the others, wicking away the moisture from her clothing.

"Do they know we're here?" Jun cast a longing look up at house and buildings.

The single window still glowed with light, but the house seemed still. Yet Luella had the feel of cords swinging, or burning, which made no sense. She wrenched her thoughts away and laid a hand over her breastbone to focus on the invisible cord connecting her to the talisman.

"If not, they may soon." Summer laid a finger across his lips, shaking his head at Jun. "First we unbind the earth, then we deal with the people, and find your uncle." He turned to Luella, waving for her to take the lead.

Everyone stepped back, giving her room.

"This way." A light mist hung in the air, floating on a gentle breeze. The storm lurked just off shore, minute lightning flickers reflecting off waves rising ever higher now that the canoes had beached.

Soft grass, mowed so short that the blades still mourned their loss, covered a wide flat swathe of ground. At the far end, overgrown bushes nearly concealed a thin path. Leaves and branches scratched Luella as she forged her way along the trail toward a small stone building set several feet above the shoreline.

Flat stones formed a half-circle in front of the building. Despite scraggly greens growing through gaps between the stones, it offered enough space for them all to gather.

Whitish stones partly covered in lichen and a dull metal door formed the front of the building, which was only a little taller than it was wide. The sides and gently slanted roof were made of darker gray stones. There were letters and numbers, words and dates, engraved into the stone.

The younger Deyo pushed ahead of the rest, running gentle fingers over the carvings. He turned around, gaze going first to his father. "It's a tomb. The first Whistles are buried here."

"The talisman is in there." Luella hung back, huddling close to May and Jun. After her earlier experience, she had no desire to disturb the dead and go in.

For a long moment, no one else stepped forward. Only the Deyos went close enough to the tomb to touch the sides.

"They're my ancestors,"—the older Deyo rubbed his chin. "I'll get it, whatever it is. Part of my penance for not believing my . . . for not investigating for so long."

"Our ancestors," his son said.

The Deyos exchanged a long glance. The elder nodded. Father and son wrestled with the door, which refused to move. The hinges didn't even creak.

"Brother?" Summer stretched out a hand toward Runner. The younger man sighed.

"Allow me." Runner joined the Deyos. "I have a whisper of earth speaking."

He set his palm against the metal. A moment later, the door opened and he leaped back, his face scrunching in horror.

A thick, sickly sweet odor rolled out, causing everyone to draw back. Luella buried her mouth and nose in the crook of her elbow. Coughs and thick swallows came from all directions around.

The air speaker gestured, turning in a circle, and a great gust of wind swooped in and out. The stench grew worse for a moment, then ebbed without ever quite going away.

The elder Deyo lifted his top and pulled it over the lower half of his face, revealing a small, pale potbelly. He fumbled, trying to tie the cloth tight, until his son did it for him. Then returned the favor.

"Where do we go?" The cloth muffled the man's voice.

"In and to the right." Luella coughed as she lowered her arm and tried to breathe only through her mouth. "I'll tell you when you're close."

"That's not necessary." The older Deyo paused in the doorway. "I think I see it. There's something glowing."

Luella covered her ears against the sounds coming from the tomb, but couldn't not know the grunts and groans and thuds as father and son retrieved a necklace from their ancestress.

The elder exited the tomb with his arm straight out, holding the talisman as far away as he could. Lightning glinted on the gold chain wound across his fingers. Below, a luminescent green stone with a hollow swayed with his every footstep. His face was almost as green as the stone.

His son pulled the tomb door shut behind, latch catching with a solid click.

The wind returned, whipping around and carrying away the last of the putrid stench. Damp breezes remained, tossing the stone this way and that until a faint rumble rippled through the earth and stones. Luella swayed, grabbing hold of May and Jun to little purpose since they, too, struggled for footing until the rumble ended.

The air lay still around them, every single breeze having vanished.

The older Deyo turned to the binders.

Summer took the stone, holding it in cupped hands and letting the chain fall through his fingers. Smoke laid her hands over his. Muttered words escaped them as they whispered together.

Luella lifted her head, as movement in the distance impinged on her senses. Things breaking, being torn apart, and fire burning. Across the flagstones, Vic too had his head up and a puzzled expression.

"This was a gift from the earth," Summer said.

Smoke drew back, letting the glowing stone be seen in the cup of his hands. She said, "It cannot be bent or broken. We must determine the proper way to return it."

"Then what do we do?" Jun asked. "Where is my uncle?"

His question had nothing to do with the stone or unbinding the earth, yet it resonated in Luella. Footsteps in the distance, but drawing close, resonating with the stone. Two, maybe three people, all connected.

"Do nothing, yet," she said. "We wait for them."

Before anyone could ask who, a ghostly woman appeared at the end of the path and laid a finger across her lips.

Eyes of fire glowed in the dark behind her.

PART FIVE
AUGUSTA DEYO

CHAPTER 21

THE SLIPPERY SLOPE

How many days since Augusta arrived at Sanctuary Hall?

She lay curled on her left side atop a thick mattress cocooned within soft cotton sheets and a blue and green star quilt to keep out the early morning chill. Her head remained on the down pillow roughly where she'd settled at the start of the night, but her limbs were pinned to her torso within her long linen nightgown and the covers that were no longer tucked under the sides or bottom of the bed. She'd tossed and turned until her toes were uncovered and a tiny chill gust sneaked up her legs.

The gray light of early dawn angled through the half-open windows. She'd pulled the curtains wide before bed, the better to lie and gaze out at the dark starry sky above. No stars gleamed now, as faint hints of pink began to streak through the gloom. She'd been given one of the smaller guest chambers, containing only a single bed, small bureau, and washstand. It was painted pale green and decorated with a pine theme: the paintings on the walls bore pine trees; the bowl on the washstand had a pine tree at the bottom; and even the rug was woven with a pine tree pattern.

Despite the late hour at which she'd sought her bed, she'd slept enough. No one stayed up that late at the Hall; no matter how enjoyable the games, they usually wrapped up by midnight. The recent arrival of Cousin Susanna's sister and her family had increased the numbers enough that they'd played several games of murder—with every light in the house put out, except in the servants' quarters —as players wandered the halls waiting for the randomly selected murderer to strike.

Such fun. Augusta hadn't laughed as much since the previous night's games and the night before that, and . . .

Frowning, she struggled to sit up. Untangling herself required wiggling and pulling and far more time than she'd have thought, she'd got herself that compacted.

Yet by the end, when she sat panting on the edge of the bed with her nightgown hiked up to her thighs and feet dangling, she still hadn't calculated the number of days.

She'd swum in the lake for the first time two days after her arrival. Or was that three? Then again, perhaps the day her cousins had taken her sailing was before the first swim, though it could be after. The current guests were surely the first batch to stay, other than Augusta, but there might have been day visitors?

Sliding off the bed, she pulled open the top drawer of the bureau and retrieved the letter from her father. That would give her a date to count from, since the actual day she'd come had slipped from memory. Except, for a moment the crisp papers stuck together but the folds didn't align so they separated into two letters. In the second, dated three days after the first, her father had expressed pleasure that she was enjoying her time away. *You deserve a vacation,* he'd written. *Take another week by all means. Your brothers and I can wait until you get home to hear about all your adventures.*

Adventures. Today would bring another. Her belly growled, as much in anticipation as hunger.

Dark clouds loomed in the distance across the lake, as they had every morning without ever quite turning into a storm. It had rained three times since her arrival, at least. One full day and two afternoons, plus the night before given the cool, damp smell floating in through the window.

Augusta pulled on an old comfortable pair of skirt-pants and a long tunic, both in green. The room must be getting to her. A quick run or two through her hair with a comb, and she was off to the breakfast table.

Only George and his son, George Whistle, V, better known as Quint, were there, both dressed in casual clothes and sandals and drooped over big mugs of coffee despite plates of steaming scrambled eggs and bacon. The oval table had plenty of places set, and warm foods kept in chafing dishes along the buffet at the far end. Pale yellow wallpaper decorated with flowers and vines, plus two east-facing windows pouring in sun, made the room a cheery place.

"Are you ready?" George asked.

"Absolutely." Augusta selected a slice of buttered toast and a cup of jasmine tea, to ease her nerves.

"Are you sure about this?" Quint scowled, a younger, taller version of his father in all things except preference for shorts over lightweight pants.

"It'll be fine." George bumped elbows with his son, and the younger man's face cleared.

They managed to clear their plates and mugs. Augusta finished her tea, but ate only half the toast.

Quint headed off one way, while George and Augusta left through a side door from the family parlor. It had the best view of the gradual slope down to the beach and shore.

George had spent the past days dashing this way and that, always promising Augusta a longer, more involved visit with the speakers but never managing to deliver—until, the night before, he'd pledged to devote the entire morning to her.

The lake stretched out, waves and water flashing as they reflected sunlight nearby. The clouds hadn't moved, forming a nearly perfect crescent around the Hall. Sweet-scented breezes danced across the grassy lawn, but stiff breezes blew higher—a group of three hawks fought to reach the trees along the lake's north shore.

"Do you ever take the speakers to wade in the lake?" Augusta asked.

"We'd lose them." George led Augusta the long way around the house.

"Even the air speakers?"

"They don't seem interested in water, other than what they need to drink to survive." He frowned and shook a finger at the dark clouds. "I blame that on them."

A gravel drive formed a circle in front of the main door to the house, originating in the dirt road that swept off around the eastern end of the lake. A large swathe of land on this side of the lake belonged to the Hall. When the convoy had arrived, way back when, they'd passed cottages for laborers and fields for crops, horses, and other animals. All lay around the bend of the hill. This side was for the house and gardens, and the speakers' dwellings.

A sizable mass of vegetation grew along the lake shore with slabs of stone forming a peak at the far side. Overgrown bushes and weeds intermingled with whip-thin lengths of grass and gray stones.

"What's that?" Augusta stopped and bent to peer at one of the stones. The weathered surface might once have had carving, but only a few lichen-covered curves remained.

"The old burying ground." George tapped Augusta's back to urge her along.

"Graves? You leave them like that?" Augusta blinked. The view before her wavered for a moment, between blurry and clear and back.

"We have to." George sighed, kicking at a clump of grass. "I can only afford so many gardeners, and the ground is witched in some way. Every time we've gone through and trimmed things, it's grown back in a matter of hours. We need an earth speaker to come and work things out, but on the occasions I've gotten one out here, they've babbled about ghosts and run away."

"Who's buried there?" Augusta asked, remembering the small stone building she'd seen from across the lake when on the way, a week and a half earlier. Yes, that was how long!

"The first generation of Whistles here in the crypt, and some of their servants in graves, but no one has been buried here for decades, centuries. Even my grandparents chose to be buried in the city cemetery, where I'll be someday." George scooped Augusta's hand and tucked it around his elbow, as though they were at a formal occasion. "But don't you want to see more of the speakers?"

As they curved around, they left the graves—and thoughts of them, behind.

"What you need to understand is that Sanctuary Hall is not cheap to run in the way it deserves," George said.

That Augusta easily believed. The number of house servants alone had to run up quite a high figure.

"And housing and caring for the speakers is very expensive," George continued.

"But the State covers that," Augusta said.

"The State contributes money, but it doesn't come anywhere near to paying for all that's needed." He sighed and rubbed his forehead. "I've argued until I was hoarse to every state agency involved, but to no avail. They think what we're doing is no more complicated than running an asylum or sanatorium, and there are so many other folk with their hands out asking for money for this public health problem or some mental health nonsense. The government doesn't understand the dangers of caring for speakers capable of calling the elements."

"But everyone at the Institute says the State stipends suffice." Augusta blinked, vision blurring again. She shivered. "Even Father once said they seemed outright generous, likely because the Governor doesn't want the havoc they could cause in a city."

"Your father knows intellectually that we have to take great care, as before we started bringing the uncommunicative speakers here, he lost two who jumped out the windows. The winds took them, but who knows where. But he hasn't thought the implications all the way through." George grasped Augusta's hands. "I'm hoping you'll keep from jumping to conclusions. Let me lead you through, and then maybe you can help explain it to him someday."

"Of course." It made sense. What seemed enough in the city could easily be insufficient in practice. Another blink, and Augusta's vision returned to normal. "Then how do you make up for the gap?"

"We ask the speakers to help fund their own care."

Hinges groaned as George pulled open a door in the center of a stone wall.

He led the way into a small courtyard with stone walls and floor, but no ceiling. It should have been warmer, with the walls blocking the light wind, but several chilly gusts danced unpredictably around. One minute a trill of air raised goose bumps along Augusta's arms, then shifted to run down her spine, then off somewhere else.

A short man stood in the center of the courtyard, head bowed and hands bound together behind his back. An old white smock hung loosely from shoulders to knees, light against creamy gold skin and short black hair. The same speaker who'd come with the convoy from Albany after a few months at the Institute. Zhang Cheng or Cheng Zhang, Augusta had never been quite clear which name was which. An air and earth speaker, as she recalled, but air had come to predominate.

His gaze flickered her way, but he said nothing. Did nothing. His head turned slightly, following the progress of a gray-clad servant busy laying odd-shaped pieces of canvas or burlap in circles around Zhang while another in slightly brighter clothes watched from a corner.

One blink later, and Augusta recognized the cloth was in fact empty bags with their mouths agape.

A second blink, and the servant in the corner turned out to be Quint.

"What is this?" Augusta bent and touched one of the bags. A shock snapped from the fabric to her skin, the brief bright blaze impossible to miss and nearly blinding. There was nothing in the bags, but evidently some magic had been worked into the cloth. She rose, cupping her aching hand, although the skin showed no sign of injury.

"The speakers take turns helping pay their way. This is

Zhang's time to contribute. You'll see and understand soon." George positioned Augusta in the corner opposite his son, where she could watch with ease—as long as she stayed as he put her. "Watch and learn."

Her concerns faded away as George picked a careful path through the empty bags to face Zhang. The servant who'd laid them out grabbed Zhang, holding him straight.

"Call the winds." George stared at Zhang.

The speaker resisted, tried to look away. Breezes whipped around the enclosed space, tugging at every bit of loose clothes and hair. Despite the sun pouring down, the winds brought an icy chill.

Augusta quaked.

Then all at once, the speaker's body bowed over. The breezes spiraled around the courtyard, going every way at once. Strands of hair blew across Augusta's face, sticking to her damp skin. She shook her head, trying to clear her vision.

One by one, bags puffed up as gusts whirled into them.

It required several orders by George and Quint for Zhang to summon winds to fill all the bags.

George and Quint walked around pulling the drawstrings one by one. Each bag remained full, the sides shifting and twisting, but the trapped air couldn't escape.

The courtyard turned warm. Sweat sheened on Augusta's skin, and her shirt and pants stuck to her skin. She pushed her hair away from her face, tucking the slick strands behind her ears with shaky hands.

Zhang crouched on the stones, shoulders shaking. He lifted his head long enough to cast one glance Augusta's way. His dark glaze blazed through her, accusing or pleading or . . .

George passed between them, giving each an approving

nod, and Augusta shivered but stayed in place. Her muscles twitched, and she leaned more of her weight against the sturdy wall.

More gray-clad servants appeared. Two carried Zhang away while others helped Quint load the dancing bags onto a red wagon.

Only for another air speaker to be brought in, this time a light-complexioned man in his twenties who'd once been a friend of Jake's, and after him a similar man. Twice more empty bags were laid out around bound speakers, who summoned air spirits to fill them.

George squeezed her shoulder as he helped her stumble from her corner. Her feet and legs ached pins and needles for holding still so long.

"That's the first part done, though there's more do." George guided Augusta out, following the track taken by the wagon over to a barn, its green-and-brown sides matching the hillside well enough that Augusta hadn't noticed it before.

"What . . ." She didn't know what to ask, just waited for what he'd tell her.

"The speakers bring air spirits or water spirits, which we keep in bags or bottles accordingly." As they entered the dark, cool shade of the barn, he waved at the shelves heaped high with bags of air and bottles of water. "Then Quint and I set bindings on the spirits to power autowagons. We ship the bags and bottles out to cities and sell them. The money, less expenses, comes back here to support the speakers."

"Oh, that . . . makes sense." Though it also made her head hurt, and her legs and feet still ached. George helped her sit on a stool to one side and watch as the servants moved the newest bags to the shelves.

"It's hard work, even shared with my son." George sighed. "But binding runs in our family. The Deyos have no magic, which I always thought why your father's gift for binding is so weak, except yours is not. I was wondering, hoping . . . since you're a binder, too, will you help?"

Her mouth opened and the answer came out without thought, exactly fitting to what he'd shown her, and the clear need for additional funds to support the speakers and the Hall.

"Of course."

CHAPTER 22
DROWNING DEEPER

Mother visited Augusta's dreams. Augusta knew she slept, for her mother hadn't changed at all. Her tall, lithe figure first appeared in the distance as though ready to go to church: dark-brown hair scarcely touched with gray braided and piled high in a coronet atop her pale oval face, impeccably clad in a cream blouse with ample lace matched with a flowing blue skirt. With every breathy half-step drawing nearer, Mother came a little more undone. Braids slipped, then cascaded down her back. Her cream blouse became untucked, the lace tattered, and the skirt shifted to stained skirt-pants decidedly not meant for public occasions.

But she was still Mother, still twitchy and apt to totter on her toes when excited.

Augusta ran to meet her, nightgown flowing loose around her calves and ankles. They met and for one long moment squeezed tight. Warmth and rightness flooded Augusta head to toe.

Until Mother stepped back. Her fingers slid down Augusta's arms to catch and grip.

Then even that was lost. Mother's mouth opened without making a sound, even to breathe. Eyes widened, head tilted back, and then she fell to her knees. Her expression pleaded with Augusta for something.

Augusta couldn't speak any more than her mother. Only sight and touch existed in this misty gray dream.

Sight, touch . . . and change.

Mother vanished. In her place, in her exact posture kneeling and face upturned with a pleading, haunted expression, was Zhang. Just as he'd been the day before, or however many days before.

His mouth shaped a word. Even without sound, Augusta couldn't mistake it: help.

Augusta started awake, covered in sweat and sheets damp. Even the quilt took some of the moisture pouring off her. Her heart pounded so hard it seemed to want to leap from her breast. Every muscle in her body ached as she panted and struggled for breath. She sat up and rocked back and forth, arms wrapped across her chest.

Darkness surrounded her, only a few chilly gleams of moonlight easing the deep of night. A cool draft filtered through the window left ajar again, though she should've known better. How many nights had she gone to bed warm and woken chilled in the early morning air? As many nights as she'd been here, and she still had trouble numbering those.

Pushing the covers aside, she stumbled out of bed. Her toes rose away from the cool floorboards. She grabbed hold of the edge of the bed, panting slowing and heartbeat easing, and spent a minute or three fumbling for her slippers which she'd somehow kicked half-under the bed. Another, and she'd grabbed the soft robe hanging from the back of the door and belted it over her nightgown. She stumbled down the hall to the bathroom to drink from cupped hands and wash sweat from her face.

Back in her bedroom, she flapped the sheets and remade the bed, but couldn't bear to lie down just yet.

The draft twined around her ankles, so she went to the window and shut it—only to stay with her hands on the frame.

Light clouds hovered overhead, parting only in a few places to allow moonbeams to seep through. Yet that was true only of the grounds and a little way out into the lake. Beyond loomed the same storm as every day. Sometimes portions of it went around the Hall while gentle rain fell overhead, but the bulk always remained.

Something moved on the waves. She pressed her cheek against the glass and held her breath. A boat bobbed in the waters, dark but differently arranged than the shifting waves. A canoe? Several people were in the boat, but she couldn't manage an exact count. Three or four.

It roughly paralleled the shore, then turned away.

Even as it did, a faint silver light flared in the center of the lawn.

A woman stood there, glowing silver but dressed in the fashion of several centuries back with wide skirts and a tight, flat bodice. Despite the distance and dark, she was transparent with the movement of waves visible through her upper half.

An actual ghost! Father had said the Hall was haunted, but Augusta hadn't thought *she*'d see a specter.

Her gasp broke the silence in the room. The ghost surely couldn't hear across the distance, but nevertheless the spectral woman waved. A moment later, she headed down the path that George had said led to the old burying ground.

Augusta remained at the window for a while longer, but nothing more strange occurred. She kept her robe on when she finally retreated to her cool bed and mostly dry sheets.

As she lay curled on her side, not quite ready to start counting sheep, she hoped for no more dreams.

Though she wouldn't mind seeing her mother again.

CHAPTER 23

WATER, GHOST, AIR

Augusta talked herself out of having seen the ghost. It was nothing more than a hallucination brought on by the incipient headache pounding at her temples when she woke. After all, why would Augusta see a ghost *here* when she never had before, despite the number of ghosts reputedly haunting parts of Albany?

The headache left her disinclined to talk at breakfast early in the morning, despite having only George and Quint for company again. Everyone else seemed bent on sleeping in most mornings, parents and teenagers alike. Augusta considered remaining in her room, but rest proved elusive and so she'd risen, dressed casually, and headed down to drink citrus juice and consume whatever fruit was on offer: this morning a mix of berries.

To her relief, George took one look at her and decided that she might watch him and Quint work with the water speakers to bottle spirits, but would not help in the process. He'd start her two days later when they worked with air speakers again.

"We take them in turns, so everyone gets two days

217

minimum between shifts. We don't want to strain them," George assured Augusta later, in the soggy, humid courtyard as his son and a servant capped the bottles.

Augusta nodded, turning away from the third and last speaker kneeling in the center. Although the woman was closer in age to Augusta than Augusta's mother, her hunched posture was far too reminiscent of the nightmare before.

And the ghost.

Who Augusta hadn't seen, whether or not she existed.

Yet all the same, when the family gathered on the lawn late afternoon for a game of croquet, Augusta tipped her straw hat at them and bowed out. She smiled at the mix of generations, from George's aunt and uncle on his mother's side representing the silver-haired contingent down to George's younger daughter and his cousin's youngest son, in their early teens. All of whom got along to a stunning degree with only minor flares of temper.

They offered gentle murmurs of protest at her declining to participate, but accepted it with good grace after the second refusal.

A light breeze blew high and soft white clouds floated in the sky, occasionally blocking the sun. A storm loomed over the lake, but that was usual by now.

The whack of mallets against wooden balls, with the requisite cries of joy or grief over where the balls went and what or who they struck, provided an aural backdrop to her meanderings around the edges of the lawn. Her headache had mostly receded to an occasional throbbing, but the repeated whacks didn't help.

So she wandered further afield, farther from the lawn— and stumbled across a faint trail through the overgrown vegetation. It was little more than a narrow path where someone had trodden over long grass and pushed through bushes just enough to leave evidence of their passage—and a relatively clear way forward.

A few feet in, the trail split. One section curved this way and that, and the other offered a relatively straight shot to the small stone building back against the hillside.

The tomb. Of course. George had mentioned this was the old burying ground.

Augusta followed the twisting trail. It was less trodden. Indeed, the grasses and brush depressed with crunches and groans under her shoes as though she was the first to pass this way.

The curves led her from stone to stone, most unmarked and none larger than the span of two hands. If these marked graves, the diggers had not maintained even the illusion of burial in straight lines.

Except for the tomb. The door was closed, and she didn't approach close enough to touch the latch—only enough to read the inscription on the plaque to one side. The tomb itself was made of gray stones similar to the building blocks used for the Hall, and likely quarried nearby. They showed signs of weathering, and lichen grew on the shadier side.

In contrast, the plaque was made of white stone, though old enough to accrue dirt in the engraved letters. The words proclaimed this the burial place of the founders of the Whistle family, offering a brief and highly edited history that made no mention of the earliest Whistle running from Charles II.

If the family was in the tomb, who was buried in the graves? Perhaps servants.

The whole definitely needed better care. She turned

away to follow the straight track to the lawn—only to freeze and glance back at the tomb.

As a cloud passed before the sun, silvery lines danced against the door, forming the outline of a woman's face and hands pressed as though trying to escape.

Then the cloud moved on, and the lines vanished.

In the same fashion the day's events blurred together, and into every other day, as Augusta lay in bed wondering, again, how long she'd been at the Hall. It was all wonderful —good company, good fun, good food—but little stood out that day or the next.

Until the morning she returned to the speakers' courtyard with George at her side.

Once again, servants laid empty bags in a circular pattern on the flagstone expanse. A brisk wind blew high over the walls, but within the air was mostly still and somewhat cool as the sun had yet to burn off the night's chill.

Augusta wore a light jacket over her shirt and shorts, but goosebumps lined her legs. They doubled in number or size when a husky young male servant brought Zhang in and set him at the center of the pattern. The older man blinked and gazed around as if this were his first time, though she'd seen him there *her* first day.

"Now, get close enough to touch him." George led Augusta to the small open space at the center, right next to Zhang. He positioned her opposite the speaker, taking care to place his steps between piles of burlap. "I prefer holding the chin for something like this. It lets you look into their eyes and watch as they accept your orders and move to action."

"Touch him?" Augusta shivered as Zhang's face turned her way with a blank expression.

"Touch is essential for binding others, unless you know someone very well or are telling them to do something they want to do anyway and just need a little nudge. The speakers need a more definite push, so skin to skin is best." He patted her shoulder, then helped her cup her hand around Zhang's chin even when the speaker tried to recoil.

The older man's skin was soft and warm to the touch, warmer than her chilly fingers. He trembled, but his expression remained blank. The taut muscles along the underside of his jaw twitched as he swallowed.

"Feel the connection between you." George moved behind Augusta, bracing her with hands on her shoulders and bending to whisper in her ear. His voice was thready, sounding tired.

Connection?

It was just all strange—standing so close to anyone. She rarely came so near even her father and brothers, except for the occasional hug. Much as she enjoyed embraces, she preferred space between her and other people. An arm's length or more, so as to have room to move and breathe.

With George behind and Zhang in front, tremors rippled through Augusta's body and every nerve jangled. Zhang's pulse leaped under her fingers.

And suddenly there it was: connection. A warm sensation rippled through her, as though she petted the softest, silkiest cat ever.

"You've got it." George pulled back, and Augusta's tremors eased.

Though not her nerves.

"Now what?" she asked.

"He needs your help because he's so far gone. Tell him what to do and use the connection to make sure it takes." George eased away from her, stepping with care between the bags until he retreated to a corner. He leaned against the wall, yawning.

"Just tell him to have breezes fill the bags," Quint said from the wall, following his words with a grunt.

Augusta's hand grew warmer where she cupped Zhang's chin. She drew in a deep breath and repeated the phrase with a squeak at the end.

Nothing happened.

"Use the connection," George said.

Another deep breath. Augusta gripped tighter, wincing in echo when Zhang recoiled.

"Call the breezes. Fill the bags." This time she sent the intent down the connection between them even as she spoke.

Zhang jerked. His eyes shut and tension radiated from him.

Again, no winds whipping around the courtyard to fill the bags.

"Let me show you." Quint pried Augusta's fingers off Zhang's chin, bumping her from the center of the courtyard.

She stumbled back to take the corner he'd stood in, massaging her hand. Cold filled her, surrounded her, to the point she almost expected her breath to fog up as she exhaled.

Quint barely waited for Augusta to turn around and watch before he gave the same order.

With nothing more to show for it.

Augusta's breath caught, coming in jagged ins and outs. Relief and disappointment warred within her as George frowned and talked with Quint through several more attempts before they had Zhang taken away.

As the speaker left the courtyard, Quint wrinkled his

nose. "Isn't he the one we've been asked to send back to Albany?"

"We'll have to figure out what's going on first. They'll just have to wait." George shook his head, then turned a tired smile on Augusta. "Let's try another. Someone a bit more cooperative. Are you game?"

"I guess."

George had to coax Augusta back out into the center of the circle as a young woman about Augusta's age, but with a vacant expression on her pale face, was brought in and positioned opposite her. Blank blue eyes gazed at Augusta as George helped her stand opposite and grasp the speaker's chin again.

The woman's skin was cool to the touch, rather like sticking one's hand into a cold box.

Once again, Augusta reached for the connection between them. It snapped into being after a few minutes. Her voice trembled as she gave the order, but it worked.

Breezes broke from the wind above, darting down to circle the courtyard and riffle people's hair, pulling at Augusta's bob, before filling the bags.

"Well done." George smiled and patted her on the back, and even Quint offered a grudging "good job."

Something deep inside screamed that her mother would have hated this, and her father too. Yet it all seemed so right and proper.

But this, of all the many events, she could not forget. Zhang and the woman speaker's faces, and the feel of their chins, lingered in her memory all the remainder of that long day and into the night.

CHAPTER 24

PAST CRIMES

Augusta woke panting and dripping with sweat from a second dream of her mother. Her legs tangled in the sheets, but her cover had slipped half-off the bed leaving her heated and chilled in the same moment. She leaned over the side, wrapping her fingers in the soft, quilted folds as she hefted it back and wrapped it around her shoulders as she sat up and rocked.

This time, she'd dreamed of Mother in the courtyard. Mother as the speaker Augusta had helped—commanded —to fill bags with air spirits, even though Mother would never have been there. Her gift was small, she spoke only with drops or breezelets. It was Nanette and Frank and Callie who called winds or waves.

All the same, she could arrange her fingers just so and immediately experience Mother's hands within her grasp, the strong connection between them, and Augusta telling her mother what to do.

So real, as if Mother had been there earlier.

Except . . . Augusta had held the speaker's chin, not her

hands, so why would she not dream of holding her mother's chin?

It wasn't as if Augusta had ever done anything of the kind to Mother. If she had, she'd remember.

Or would she have wanted to forget?

Her calf muscles twitched. Still wrapping the quilt around her shoulders, Augusta rose and paced the room. Step after step grounded her in the here and now—Sanctuary Hall, with Mother seven years gone.

And a ghost outside on the lawn.

Augusta leaned against the frame. The spectral woman traced a circle on the grass, leaving a faintly luminescent trail that slowly dissipated behind her, before retreating into the overgrown vegetation.

Ghosts.

Mothers in dreams of binding.

Mothers and memories of binding.

Her stomach clenched as the thought hit her hard as a load of bricks—and even worse, with the chilling awareness that it was—no! only might be!—true.

If Augusta had suppressed a memory, wouldn't that be a kind of binding, even if she'd done it to herself?

In which case, could she unbind her memories? Father had given her the training, but even he now admitted that Augusta surpassed him in unbinding and not merely because she had a stronger gift than he.

It might be a really bad idea. What else might she have forgotten? Scraps of memories of embarrassing moments and stupid, mean things she'd said and done already lingered in her brain to torment her. She had no need of further remembered pain.

So, she needed to be specific. Unbind only what she chose, drawing on experience helping binders at the Institute only undo whatever had gone wrong, and not other bindings keeping the building fixed, and the city in one place.

She wiped sweat from her forehead, drying her eyes. It was just sweat, not tears.

Still, nothing ventured nothing gained.

She'd start small.

The plan sounded good—until she threw off the quilt and looked down at herself with her magic to find her body covered in a tangled web of bindings. So many wrapped around her that they'd blurred together even as the days had. She needed better light.

Although she didn't wait to hunt her slippers, she grabbed her robe from the door and wrapped it over her. The soft fabric did nothing to hide the bindings, but gave her a hint of warmth and the comfort of home as she padded down the hall. The tiny lamp next to the bathroom was always kept lit, offering soft yellow light that gleamed on the dark floorboards.

The bathroom door clicked shut behind her and she set the latch before turning on the overhead light. The white tiles covering the floor and walls up to waist height, the smooth white porcelain fixtures, and the metal faucets reflected back the light, making the even the light green walls too bright to look at. Too much of a contrast to the gentler light outside. She covered her eyes, breathing deep, until she adjusted and saw less red when she peered through stiff fingers.

The mirror over the sink showed her as she was: hair sticking to her head, cheeks and nose bright pink, and chest heaving. Then she looked deeper.

The web of bindings covering her appeared even worse in the bright light and clear reflection. Lines after lines wrapped around her at all angles, as if she'd grabbed a ball of rope and danced around, winding the cord anywhere and everywhere about herself. Bonds crossed her face, mashing her nose against her skull, held her upper arms against her torso, and even went up-and-down from head to crotch.

So many—too many—and all knotted together. The colors blended, in various shades of reds and blues suggesting the work of two or three or more hands. Some reminded her of George or Quint, but beneath them were others redolent of her father.

If this were a well-made binding, it would have some part that could undo the whole with a single, easy pull. That was what Father taught her, what she'd read in books on bindings, even the bad ones.

Then again, bindings were between humans and the land—to keep the earth under cities from moving and destroying houses, or fix crops in place so one didn't plant and lose the harvest because it wandered into one's neighbor's field. Or a thousand different things, none of which involved fixing people so they'd do what was wanted.

But she'd been doing worse—forcing people against their will.

One of the bonds flashed and she blinked. The bindings started to fade from sight. Gritting her teeth, she leaned in closer to study them.

Of course these bindings weren't well-made. They shouldn't exist, and they'd twisted around her too much to find any one place to start.

Two choices lay before her: take the time to study the bonds and undo them one at a time or cut.

Waiting and studying risked keeping on doing whatever the bonds laid on her to do.

Cutting could be catastrophic.

But these were on *her*! Her skin crawled, goosebumps forming everywhere because who knew what they might be doing?

She grabbed with two hands, one all those she could reach across her upper chest and the other those on her face.

Let her actions with these be replicated with all the others, to remove them in one swoop.

Was it wise?

No, but Augusta's reflection vanished briefly from the mirror and was replaced or overlaid by the ghost. The specter nodded.

Hardly an endorsement, yet even as Augusta squawked in surprise she jerked and tore the bindings.

One handful first, then the other, then the rest. Steam boiled up, filling the bathroom as sure as if she'd stepped into a hot shower.

She wrapped her arms around her chest. Warm, purring sensations flooded through her as bond after bond dissolved. The newest went first, and the quickest. The oldest unfolded slowly from around her chest. She swayed and collapsed onto the floor. Her heated face pressed against cool tiles and she whimpered as memories unfurled and rewrote what she'd thought she'd known.

Not that day that cracked her heart, but the day before. Augusta had had no notion her mother was leaving.

Yet in a new memory, Augusta came home from school to find a pile of suitcases in the front hall. She'd hung up her jacket and checked her hair in the hall mirror. Nanette sat in the parlor as usual, rocking and saying nothing. Frank and Callie whispered nearby, both in good outfits. Jake wasn't anywhere to be seen or heard, Danny the same, though there was distant singing from the kitchen where the cook was at work.

Up above, clumps and thuds from the bedrooms.

Mother had been very agitated previous night, after returning from a visit to Sanctuary Hall. Both of Augusta's memories included distant sounds of her quarreling with Father after Augusta had gone to bed, despite Augusta pulling the covers up over her head.

In the new memory, Augusta snuck up the stairs light-footed to find her room in slight disarray—the top drawer of her dresser pulled out, her jewelry box missing, and an empty suitcase laid open on the bed. The interior smelled musty, and the outside was slightly wet, enough to make a damp spot on the comforter.

Across the hall, other was in her room packing a suitcase and stuffing jewelry into bags and socks and even slipping a pearl necklace into the hem of a dress. Clothes lay in a dozen different piles on the bed, a few neat and the rest as though thrown without care. Her silvering brown hair spilled down her back in a very messy braid, half-undone. Her clothes had streaks of dust, although her hands were clean.

"Mother? Whatever are you doing?" Augusta asked.

"Oh, thank God, you're here in good time." Mother rushed to grab Augusta in a fierce, tight hug. Her fingers dug deep before she let go in an instant. Red rimmed her green eyes, and tear tracks marred her pale complexion. A spot of dirt clung to one side of her button nose. "We have to leave. There's an early evening train. You will come with us, won't you?"

"What, where, why?" Augusta sank onto the edge of the bed, mattress depressing beneath her. Mother was leaving again? There'd been no word of warning.

"I can't let my babies be treated that way. I have to get them away, to be safe, but I don't want to leave you. Please, you will come?" Mother bent and grabbed Augusta's wrists, holding tight.

"I don't understand." Augusta twisted her hands so she held her mother's, all warmth and softness where their skin met. "Can't you stay, at least until Father's home? Don't just go!"

Her mother wavered. Blinked. Her lips moved, repeating Augusta's words in a soft, dazed whisper. "Stay. Don't go."

Her lips smiled, but her eyes were wide with horror.

Augusta rocked in the bathroom as the memory dissolved. Her belly hurt, everything hurt. Bad enough to live through it the first time, but now seen with her recent experience getting speakers to put air spirits in bags.

All the signs and requirements were there: physical contact, connection, and telling Mother what Augusta wanted, for her to stay.

Bent nearly double, nose practically pressing against the tiled floor, a different memory unwrapped and reminded Augusta of its existence.

Still fully dressed down to her shoes, Augusta huddled under the covers in her bedroom at home. Footsteps echoed down the stairway, then the hall, along with bangs and thuds as things hit walls. The distant sound of Mother's voice, then the front door shut.

Someone knocked on Augusta's door.

"Go away!" She pulled the blanket over her head, trying to ignore the last vestiges of the damp spot from the suitcase she'd thrown under her bed.

Instead, the door opened. More footsteps, heavier, and

a weight pressed on the side of the bed as a warm, familiar hand stroked Augusta's back through the covers.

He said nothing, just waited.

Drawing in a deep breath, Augusta flung back the covers. "*You just let her go?*"

"I asked her to stay, to trust me to find some other way to care for our children, for Nanette." Father sighed. "I believe the best chance we have is the work we're doing at the Institute, studying magic and figuring out which speakers live the longest, healthiest lives and why. But she insisted the way we're caring for them now is horrific and she wouldn't, she couldn't, risk it for those she loves."

"She said she'd stay." Augusta's chest heaved as tears began streaming down her face.

Her father's pain was easier to see in hindsight than at the time, when Augusta had recognized little but her loss. "You bound her to stay. I don't have your power, but unbinding almost always requires less force than binding."

"She's gone? Already? Not even a day?"

"She's afraid." Father laid an arm around Augusta's shoulders, cuddling her against him and laying his head atop hers.

Augusta had taken that at first to mean Mother feared what might happen to Nanette, Frank, and Callie, until other meanings dawned.

Full realization that her mother left without her sent Augusta into a frenzy of crying over loss and guilt for the binding and that making the loss happen sooner.

Her father tried ease her. In the end, he took the simplest route to give her peace. Asking her first, and reminding her that she could undo it anytime, he laid a binding on her to forget her part in her mother's departure until she was ready.

She'd agreed then, unwilling to bear knowing that her mother sped her departure because she was afraid of Augusta working a stronger binding to make her stay.

Augusta was not sure she'd agreed now.

Regardless, no wonder her father had insisted Augusta become an expert at unbinding.

Unbinding.

Binding.

How had Augusta missed thinking about Nanette and Frank and Callie when seeing the speakers in their chains and ropes? When *Augusta* had forced one to imprison air spirits in bags?

She fumbled to her knees and bent over the toilet throwing up every last bit of food or liquid. Her whole body rebelled at the memories of what she'd done. She'd committed crimes against speakers and spirits. Sheer humanity and decency should have her reporting the cruelty and ensuring the spirits were freed.

Yet she'd taken every word George offered as truth, accepted his every rationale.

He'd bound her, just as he'd bound the speakers and spirits, albeit to different purposes.

A serious mistake, for Augusta was an expert unbinder.

CHAPTER 25

BINDING OR UNBINDING

Augusta froze at a sharp rap on the bathroom door. Warm water trickled out of the faucet over her shaky hands. Her face had a greenish cast, and the taste of bile lingered on her tongue. She'd splashed water on her hair, but it desperately needed a good brushing. Despite flushing, the smell of vomit lingered. Her nightgown and robe had escaped splashing but picked up a layer of dust from the floor. No matter how assiduous, the maids couldn't keep up with all the people using the bathroom.

She swallowed, grimacing, then called, "just a moment!"

"Augusta? Are you all right?"

George. Why would he be up in the middle of the night? He had drunk a lot at dinner, but the timing made Augusta tense. Her arms pressed tight against her sides as she turned the water off.

Could a binder feel the undoing of bonds they'd wrought? Nothing in the literature or the interviews she'd sat in on at the Institute suggested it. Once done, bindings were separate from the person who formed them—that partly explained the tangle that had covered her, as he'd added on layer after layer.

She tied the belt around her robe tighter, stood straight, and took a deep breath. "I'm fine."

When she opened the door, George stood in the hall, leaving little room to pass. He hadn't changed out of his evening attire, but the white shirt and tan pants clung to his skin and dripped onto the hall. His hair was plastered to his head and not with sweat. Even his eyelashes were slick against his skin. A wet trail on the floor showed his progress from the stairs over to the bathroom, though he'd removed socks and shoes and stood in wet, hairy bare feet.

"Are you okay?" she asked.

"The bridge is out, and some of the fields are flooding." He pulled the hem of his shirt out and wrung it, only realizing a moment later that he'd done it in the hall. His unusually pale face made the dark lines and bags under his eyes more pronounced.

"It's raining enough to flood?" How had Augusta not noticed the weather change, given how long the storm had lurked over the lake without crossing the Hall. She'd gotten too used to the strangeness.

"Oh, not here. It's only cloudy over the Hall, and everything's built high enough we're safe. Even if the lake rises another few feet, we'll only lose the beach, though Grandmother loved that beach, and sand isn't cheap to buy or have delivered." He winced, but stayed right in front of the doorway. "We had to move the horses, though, and help clear valuables from one of the lower cottages. Quint's still out there, but he sent me back. Said I was too tired to be sensible and not get trod on."

"Well, don't let me get in your way." Augusta couldn't

pass without brushing him. She didn't want a touch, not even a pat on the shoulder or arm, now that she understood how important touch was to laying bindings on humans.

George squinted at her as she tried to wriggle through and moved just enough to let her pass—except he braced an arm on the frame. She had to duck under to get out.

The instant she squeezed out, she started backing up toward her room.

"What's wrong?" he asked.

"Nothing," she shrugged, "I just had a bad dream."

"Nightmares aren't allowed here." He backed just far enough into the bathroom to wring out his clothes and have the water trickle along the tiles. A lot of moisture had already dripped onto the hall, but his hands worked away at his shirt hem. "My grandmother would always wake if I had one when I visited. She'd come into my room in the middle of the night and sit with me and stroke my back and forbid me to have any more as long as she was around. You wouldn't think it, but that always worked. I've always told my family that this is a special place, that bad dreams aren't permitted. I'm so sorry that I didn't make that true for you."

His last words hit hard. *Make that true.* Forbid nightmares, no doubt through bindings, well-meant but so wrong. Had his grandmother—Augusta's great-grandmother—done that to him? Or he'd merely interpreted it as such?

"Let's get you back to bed and see if I can do what she did." He grabbed a towel and slung it around his neck, squelching out into the hall.

Augusta scurried down, keeping an arm's length away, but his longer legs allowed him to arrive at her room at nearly same time. Both reached for the doorknob, and she recoiled.

"It wasn't just a nightmare, was it?" He looked her over with growing horror. "What have you done?"

"Shouldn't that be me asking you?" Augusta raised her hands, palms out.

"You're . . ." He waved at her body, staring at her midsection in particular. "It's all missing."

"I only undid things you did first." She lifted her chin. Why bother trying to conceal her unbound condition? "You bound me, without asking first." At least her father had asked, although that binding had lasted far too long.

"I didn't hurt you."

"That's not what I said." Augusta shook her head, swallowing hard. No matter how she tried to keep the pain back, it escaped. "Why?"

"I just made things easier."

"For you."

"For you," George said. "If I didn't, you might have taken longer to understand. Made a fuss. You'd have come to the right conclusions in the end, I just shortened the process."

Augusta's mouth hung open. She shut it with a snap, blinking away tears. Did he really believe that?

"And now we'll have to go through all the fuss and bother and explanations." He waved and blew a heavy sigh.

"You're forcing speakers to imprison elementals, and selling the spirits!" Augusta kept well back from him, the door to her room lying ajar. She could dash in and shut it behind before he could get her. Probably. But she wanted to know as much of *why* as she could get out of him first, when he was tired enough to be honest, and loose lipped.

Despite their voices rising, and echoing slightly down the hall, no doors opened. Either people were listening in their beds, or sleeping through.

George wanted to help her avoid nightmares. Had he done the same for others?

"This is exactly the conversation I was trying to avoid." He rubbed his forehead. "You're just like your mother—she wouldn't listen either."

"You've been doing this that long?" Augusta sagged against the side of the hall.

"I only started bagging and bottling spirits for the autowagon market a few years ago. It was Quint's idea." George shook his head. "No, your mother didn't like the chains and ropes keeping speakers with us. She told me we should let them be free and give them reasons to stay with us, make them care more about staying than going with the elements, though how she'd know when she never studied the matter . . . she was talking all nonsense."

"She typed all Father's notes and helped write his articles." That was one of the first things Augusta had learned to do to help after she left.

"There are reasons your father doesn't keep degrading speakers at the Institute."

"Degrading?" She no longer wanted to hear his excuses. The more he talked, the less she'd ever known him, or thought she had. It seemed to be all bindings, all pretense, the whole time she'd spent at the Hall and all their encounters back in Albany before.

"They can't talk to anyone, or they won't. Same difference. And they don't bring in enough money to pay for their housing, much less keeping this up," he stroked the wall. "Philanthropists would rather give money to the Institute —if they give any to us—but to study them not to keep them housed and fed. Quint and I just put the two together."

He'd been inching closer. Did he think she didn't notice?

"You don't have to help, but you will *not* stand in my way." He grabbed her wrist, fingers digging into skin and muscles.

But she was ready, dissolving his binding even as he set it on her.

"Unbinding is almost always easier, and faster, than binding." If he'd never heard the old adage, it was time.

And she crafted her own binding on him. Her hands filled with the soft prickle of fur—strange that binding and unbinding roused the same physical pleasure. The bonds she set would dissolve with the first touch of the morning sun, but until then she commanded him to dry himself, go to his room, and sleep and consider his choices.

By the time he woke, she'd be well into the work of undoing all that he'd done—and starting to make amends for her part.

CHAPTER 26

PRESENT WRONGS

Augusta grabbed whichever clothes were closest to hand and dressed quickly. No one would care if her yellow linen shirt was never usually worn with casual blue pants. Her fingers shook as she pulled on socks and shoes and ran a comb through her hair. It didn't matter what she looked like. Why was she so nervous, so busy procrastinating going out into the silent hall?

Exactly, the quiet hall. Her talk with George hadn't woken anyone, or her run to the bathroom before that.

Maybe George did encourage everyone to sleep well, or went further and forbid nightmares. He'd apologized for Augusta having one.

He must have bound others as well, but who? Guests? Servants? Family?

Leaving her room, she tiptoed down the hall to the master suite trying to avoid the wet footprints George had left earlier, which gleamed in the soft beams from the nightlight. Despite telling herself she could walk normally, she winced every time a floorboard creaked under her.

She laid a hand on the door and tried to sense bindings or the lack through it. Nothing.

Would he have locked the door after going to bed? He hadn't.

Her hand wrapped around the cool porcelain knob and she opened it a crack. Soft snores reached her ears despite the distance—the suite included a sitting room as well as bedroom.

Augusta's shoes sank into the thick carpet as she moved just far enough in to peer at the bedroom.

She'd never looked at humans for bindings before. Never considered there might be a need.

Then again, neither had she been aware of the binding her father laid on her, much less broken it. She'd have to talk to him about that, because it shouldn't have lasted so long even if he'd laid the condition that it end only when she was ready. He'd have done better to tell her the truth long before. Maybe that would have kept her from falling to George's bindings.

Or not.

George was guilty of binding her—but she, of all people, couldn't lay all the responsibility on him. She knew how to look for bindings, and undo them, and she'd let it happen.

Once she looked, she couldn't fail to see that Susanna was an even worse tangle of bindings, layers upon layers upon layers. No logical arrangement, no coherence, just order after order.

A sour taste bloomed in her throat, but she swallowed hard.

And forced herself to turn away. Door by door, she checked each along the hall as she passed.

Children, family, friends, everyone was plastered with

bindings in varying depths. The longer someone had known George, the more they were enshrouded.

No wonder everyone had such a lovely time here, the very kinds of enjoyment George remembered from his youth. All those stories he kept recounting, everything he'd done was to make them live again.

The layered tangles were so bad that if Augusta started undoing them one by one, she'd be lucky to get one done before morning. More likely, she'd get caught in the middle and wind up trying to explain the impossible to people who had never realized they were vulnerable.

People all too much like her. And that wasn't even counting the servants, who must also bear layer after layer to ensure they provided the setting for the good times George wanted recreated.

No, she needed to start with those who desperately required relief: the speakers.

Then the servants, and last family and friends.

Except, if she freed the speakers from the bindings, what would happen? George might well have told her the truth about loose speakers running into the lake or being carried off by winds.

Augusta didn't know what had happened to her mother or siblings or cousin. The lack of certainty, the equal possibility they were fine or in need—she'd lived years knowing she might never learn what happened or where they went. Years of wondering. She didn't want to put the families of the speakers through anything like that.

But chaining the speakers was wrong. Better to free them and let them decide what to do.

CHAPTER 27
LETTING GO

The smell of rain hung in the air, even though no drops fell. The storm seethed over the lake, as always. Tendrils wrapped around the grounds to either side, and lightning flared in the clouds, but over the Hall stretched an eerie calm. Barely even a breeze broke the stillness.

Maybe George had imprisoned too many?

Augusta stood before the door to the speakers' quarters and took a deep breath. It wasn't locked, why would it be? No one in their right mind would steal in to release the speakers—no one except her.

And she was dallying too long. Leaning her weight, she pushed the door open. The hinges squeaked. She froze for a moment, but all was quiet except a soft snore.

A lamp glowed from somewhere off to the side where she couldn't see it. Weak and pale, its beams did less to illuminate than to create shadows. The iron bedsteads turned to shadow spears on the floor. Thin, gray blankets covered mounds in seven beds.

Almost as one, a head popped up on each. Eyes glittered in the light, watching her.

None said anything, but here were the breezes missing just outside. They danced around the air speakers while personal rainclouds attended the water speakers.

Augusta stepped inside and froze at a snorting snore that dwindled into a long whistling sigh.

A narrow desk sat to one side, with an older man in a plain blue uniform slumped in a chair behind it. A watchman of some sort. She didn't recognize him from among the house servants, or those who'd dragged the speakers to the courtyard, or those who carried away the bagged and bottled spirits.

No matter.

He was covered with a thin layer of bonds, of which one had pulled loose. Augusta snuck close enough to brush a finger over it. His need for sleep had overcome the bond ordering him to remain awake, a bond George had set initially and Quint had reinforced some time back. The guard must've been exhausted, or more likely drank too much given the fumes coming off the almost-empty whiskey bottle on the floor near his slack hand.

Was there anyone around whom George, with or without Quint, hadn't bound in some way?

She wavered for a moment over whether to make him sleep until morning, but would that not be doing just what George did when a person stood—or sat—in his way?

The guard snorted and jerked, blinking and yawning. The bond trying to keep him awake glowed.

Augusta tugged just that one free, and he fell right back into sleep, lips curved in a wide smile.

Turning around, she faced the speakers. Seven still faces with wide eyes, all watching her and no one saying anything. The breezes and rain kept well away from her. If anything, the breezes flicked the scent of partly-washed bodies in her direction, that or the tang of the doorless bathroom to one side.

She pressed a finger to her lips as she walked to the center of the room. "I need you to be as quiet as possible," she said. "I'm going to untie you, unbind you. Then we'll go and free the air and water spirits in the bags and bottles, and then . . ."

In truth, she wasn't sure what would happen next. There were so many things left to be done, and only her to do them until she could free someone with influence, or get a servant to take an urgent telegram to town to get help from her father. There were so many bindings on the family and friends, and probably the staff, that should be removed with care because it would be traumatic for them. Augusta still shook now and then at the memory of yanking them off herself. She needed help.

But it was just her.

And seven speakers unable to communicate with humans.

Time enough to worry about the rest later. Rumbles of thunder suggested the storm increased, and just because it hadn't hit the Hall yet didn't mean it wouldn't.

In the nearest bed, a single flicker of lightning—small, no more than a zipping glow—ran up one of Zhang's arms and down the other.

When Augusta drew near, the lightning crackled.

Fine, she left him for last.

She nearly tripped getting away from him to the far side of the room. A woman lay in the bed, the same woman she'd ordered to imprison air spirits earlier. Augusta's age now, Nanette's back before Mother had taken her cousin away.

"I'm sorry," Augusta said. The words sounded thin in the silence.

The woman said nothing, though her eyebrows lifted suggesting she'd heard and understood. A breeze whipped through the air between the two. Then the woman tilted her head, and the breeze retreated.

The gray blanket covered the speaker's prone body. She'd lifted her head from the thin pillow. Now she raised her arms. The cover fell back on one side, but tangled in the other. Shackles hung around her wrists, but not so loose that she could get her hands out. Cords bound the shackles to the bedstead. They were tied and knotted several times over around the bed, but the end fastened to the shackle had a metal clamp.

It took a few fumbling moments for Augusta to figure out the right way to place her fingers on the clamp and unfasten it. A little pressure, then she tilted it and one arm was free if weighted down with the shackle.

The woman pulled the blanket off revealing the other wrist and the additional shackles and cords connecting ankles to the bedstead. She tossed the blanket to the breeze, which ripped it to shreds that cascaded around as Augusta set to work.

Three more clicks, and the woman was free.

One by one, Augusta removed the cords binding speakers to the bedsteads. She couldn't do anything about the shackles, but none of the speakers showed any sign of complaint. Breezes tugged at her until they realized what she was doing, and then tried to help although the cooler ones nearly froze her fingers.

The water speakers proved tougher to release, because

the metal clamps had started to rust in the rain. All but one eventually gave way, and for that last one, an air speaker who had been watching set a breeze to untie the knots. The water speaker tied the cord around his waist.

As she freed each speaker, they sat up and swiveled to put their feet on the floor. Otherwise they didn't move. Once-white smocks hung loose about their bodies, showing that their torsos faced forward—but their heads turned on their necks as they watched her go from bed to bed.

Six done, Augusta headed for Zhang.

The light behind her increased, turning pale and silvery. A cool forest scent blew away any stench of sweat or urine, though beneath the evergreen tang lay a hint of decay.

The ghost stood exactly where Augusta had a little while ago—complete with one finger across her lips signing for quiet.

The other hand the ghost extended, palm out.

"Reinforcements?" Augusta muttered to herself more than the ghost, then jerked when the ghost nodded and half-smiled.

A crackling noise behind made Augusta whirl around.

Zhang had freed himself. The lightning flickering over his body consumed the ropes. The clamps dangled from his shackles, then the metal turned red briefly and fell away, leaving a hint of smoke rising from his skin.

He was slower than the others to sit up, watching her with caution and puzzlement.

"Keep quiet," Augusta put her finger against her lips again, and the ghost mimicked her. "And we'll go free the air and water."

The speakers exchanged glances. Breezes whisked from one to another. Rain clouds merged, then separated.

All but one of the speakers rose together and formed a single line out the door, accompanied by breezes and rains.

Only Zhang remained. He stood slower, joints creaking and his gaze shifting back and forth between Augusta and the ghost.

"Are you coming?" Augusta waved at the door. He'd not obeyed earlier, no matter what Augusta or George said, although he had before. Perhaps he'd had some brain fever. Did he even understand?

The ghost's lips moved. Augusta couldn't hear anything, but Zhang smiled and headed out. As he reached the doorway, he made a gesture.

She ran, but was far behind. By the time she reached the barn holding the imprisoned spirits, the speakers had already tried ripping off the lock and settled for cracking the door. It lay ajar, half the planks bent double with ample splinters in evidence.

None of them spoke any more than they had for months, but they made up for it by eagerly ripping the bags open and smashing the bottles, paying no attention to the fact that they were barefoot amid the growing welter of broken glass.

The freed breezes mixed with those who'd accompanied the speakers to create a true wind. It tugged at their hair, ran along their hands . . .

And blared a protest when Augusta went to join the speakers. Dust blew santo her eyes. She shaded them with one arm as gust after gust pushed her back. After a few tries she stumbled back content to watch and ensure all the traps were opened.

The waters flowed together, but rather than trickling away from the building down to the lake, they formed an ever-expanding pool. The personal rainstorms dropped low, merging with the waters to double their size.

The wind whipped around the speakers, a breeze separating to twine along Zhang's shoulders then double back. The waters and wind touched, and with one accord the speakers left the building.

Zhang touched the broken door. Sparks leaped from his fingers, and the planks caught readily. The wind blew growing flames back at the building until it caught.

Augusta didn't need the wind pushing her to retreat from the intense heat pouring off the burgeoning blaze.

"Have you got them all?" Augusta asked, staying back and swaying as she tried to take in the speed with which the speakers had wrought devastation.

The water speakers nodded as one, all smiling. Holding hands, they moved to stand in the middle of the pool of freed water. It lifted them up and raced downhill, the speakers' smocks flapping as they slid toward the lake. An immense wave crashed up onto the land. The two waters met, merged, and the water speakers rode high over to the lake and vanished in the distance.

Augusta didn't expect to ever see them again.

But they were only half the freed speakers. She whirled just in time to see the great wind, made greater by never-imprisoned breezes and storm winds, lift the burning frame of the barn in one great flaming roar. It rose several feet off the ground, turning into an immense ball of flame, then dropped back down as little more than smoldering, blackened remains in the exact spot the barn had once stood.

The air speakers raised their arms and the wind swirled around them. Their heads leaned back and they smiled as the wind carried them away.

In freeing them, Augusta had condemned their families

to wonder whether they were dead or still alive somewhere with their elements. Yet the speakers had showed such joy that Augusta couldn't quite be sorry.

Even if they'd all left except Augusta and the ghost.

And Zhang.

The last flame jumped from a charred beam to dance on his hands. His skin seemed untouched, but his eyes were dark as he gazed past Augusta at the ghost. Hairs prickling along the back of her neck, Augusta turned around.

The ghost gestured for them to follow her.

Zhang did so without hesitation.

Augusta glanced at the house and other outbuildings. They showed no signs of activity anywhere, or any indication Quint had returned and found anything amiss. George had bound everyone too tight. What if there were a fire in the house at night? Or maybe he'd allowed for that in his bindings. She could check when she started freeing them.

Let them sleep for now. Tomorrow would be soon enough to bring them pain.

Drawing a deep breath, she followed Zhang and ghost across the lawn and toward the burying ground.

PART SIX
ZHANG CHENG

CHAPTER 28
FIRE

~ake, wake, wake, wake.~

Crackling warmth woke Cheng. Orange and yellow sparkles flitted along his body, swirling and twisting over every inch of him both over and under his loose smock. They warmed him to the point his skin cooled where they passed, leaving itches and him longing for their return. He twisted in a vain attempt to soothe the irritated skin, but fell short.

For a moment, in sleep, he'd forgotten that he was tied to the bed. The cords fastening his legs gave him just enough play to shift and sleep on his side or back, but he had less play with his arms. His back ached no matter how he lay on the thin mattress. The glittering points managed to squeeze between his body and the bed, and drew lines along his back. The heat helped with the hurt, but not enough.

Easy enough to see the flickers dancing over him in the deep of night, though Cheng followed their progress whether or not he could see them. Even when they passed through the limited circle of lamplight near him, he knew where they were. Warmth melted the wax from his ears, sending it running over his sheets in liquid rivulets to puddle on the floor.

No one else showed any sign of interest, or even waking. Several snores regularly broke the quiet, ranging from soft and whispery to loud honks.

A breeze whisked by, still friendly with him and other air speakers despite how many were now trapped in bags. They knew of their fellow breezes' captivity. Several times, they'd swept by Cheng's legs or arms and share the sensation of burlap against skin. But they didn't seem to hold it against him, or perhaps they hadn't put the pieces together. Breezes rarely held complex thoughts for long, unlike the greater winds created when they blended together.

Someone wept, in their sleep or waking. Probably a water speaker, for a soft rain trickled against bedding and floorboards in the same direction.

Cheng tried to reach the earth. He stretched and brushed his fingers against the iron posts supporting the bed. His body rested in air, albeit atop layers of fabric, but the posts stood on the floorboards, which surely pressed against earth somewhere.

~I'm here. I need help.~

~Safe. Secure. I have you.~ The deep earth replied, the words rote and with no indication that it had heard Cheng or responded to him.

He yelled as much as a man could without voice and movements limited. Pressed his feet hard against the bed frame, willing his fear and desperation to reach the metal and down to the earth on which it stood.

Nothing from the earth. Or air.

Only fire responded. ~Time to burn?~

Burn? Tapped in a wood building, he'd go up with the flames.

~Not you. We know the difference~ The flickers over his body warmed without singeing. ~Burn it down?~

~There are others.~ Also trapped. Cheng couldn't condemn them to burning to death, not yet.

A sense of disappointment tied with resignation impinged on him everywhere the warm sparkles passed.

The ghost manifested near him, silver light against the darkness but perhaps fainter than before. He couldn't be sure.

She said something, but the air spirits took time before carrying it to his ears. ~The time is soon. You will be ready? ~

Ready for what? He'd promised to try and convey a message for her to the deep earth, but it hardly heard him. How could he do any better bound as he was? He shrugged.

She nodded.

~Change is on the way.~ No sooner had the breeze carried her words to him than she vanished.

An instant later, the door hinges grated as it swung open. The young woman who'd accompanied their jailor earlier, the one who'd tried to force Zhang to trap breezes, entered. Her shoulders were up by her ears, her whole body hunched in. The slant of lamplight made her eyes seem deep, dark pits as she shuffled forward.

Breezes whispered as they twirled where the other air speakers lay. The fall of rain near the water speakers increased.

All snoring ended, and the change in breathing indicated the other speakers were awake.

What did the woman want?

She didn't say anything. Stopped moving, except looking around. Her breathing increased and shallowed.

Change, the ghost had said, but nothing about whether it was good or ill.

~Air, help!~

No answer.

~Earth, help!~ He pressed hard against the iron, willing the earth to understand. No matter how slow it generally moved, it could do much fast.

~Safe, safe, safe,~ the earth replied, same as before.

No point in Cheng appealing to water. Perhaps rain or the lake would listen to the water speakers, but not to him.

Only one left.

~Fire?~

~Let me in.~ The flickers combined and flattened to a single point of heat trailing over his body.

The heat suggested all manner of destruction or other protective actions. All Cheng had to do was let fire in under his skin, allow the seed of fire within to grow.

He hesitated for a moment. Fire promised danger, but better that than staying as he was. The wax had helped, but it was gone. Sooner or later his jailer would force him to trap breezes again.

~Come.~ He willed himself to open to fire. ~But start small.~

He wrapped his fingers around the cords binding his arms to the bed. They went up in smoke in an instant, and a kind breeze wafted the spiraling fumes away from Cheng. The mere brush of a finger against the cords tying his feet and they were gone too.

The clamps dangled against his manacles. Irritating, both in the sound and vibrations of metal banging metal.

The crackle of bright light and warmth wreathing his

arms didn't speak words, but made clear that fire understood restraint and could consume only what it wished—even only what *he* wished.

A blaze of heat around each wrist and ankle left his muscles wobbly. He grabbed hold of the bedposts to stay upright, the metal squashing and reforming with finger marks under his grasp.

All that, and it seemed he didn't need fire to defend against the woman after all. She'd freed the other speakers and sought to loosen also the spirits trapped in bags and bottles.

Yes!

Despite the warmth flowing along his legs, he remained wobbly. His first steps were slow and careful, but soon he raced out of the building—well behind the other speakers. Lightning flashed along his arms and legs as he ran.

Weak the other speakers might be, but they set on destruction with an eager will, and left little for him. Crisping the torn bags that had contained breezes did little to ease the anger burning within.

Fire fed on his anger, growing the seed within and promising to bring it all down.

Cheng strode into the barn, broken glass melting under his feet. He threw out his arm and fire lashed out. Fire protected him from the flame, but only his external body. Deep within, his seed of fire expanded further. The other speakers left, giving themselves over to air and water, but he remained.

~Danger!~ A daring breeze blew flames higher as it brought him the ghost's warning. ~Remember your promise. The time has come.~

To give her message to the deep earth. Would it hear him now that he'd let in fire?

Much as he longed to burn further, she'd helped him. He'd promised. He left the ashy remnants of the barn. Stood on bare earth and reached down deep.

The deep earth either didn't hear him, or didn't care. It only repeated the same litany of safety and security as before.

~Not here.~ The ghost pointed toward the lake as a breeze brought her words to him. ~Come.~

He followed the ghost, the other woman hard on his heels. Having her behind him made him twitchy. What if she tried to grab him and bind him?

Fire flared around him, a bright orange cloak flapping as he hurried along. The seed grew more.

She slowed and left several paces between them.

The ghost led him across a close-mown lawn. The grass crisped and turned to black ashes where he passed. He singed his way through overgrown bushes, though he tried to keep any from catching flame. Even in the dark night, an immense storm cloud filled with flickering lightning rumbled over the lake, mere meters off the shore at most.

A group of people crowded around a stone building. Men and women, young and old—though mostly young— and all in long two-piece bathing suits. They stood on a flat section paved with stone. Cheng's first step cracked a stone beneath him, but not the second. Fire pulled back within him, but heat flowed in his veins and his skin glowed an orange yellow much brighter than his usual appearance. A soft bolt of lightning hissed as it twisted around his head.

He didn't blame them for drawing away from him. He'd have done the same.

Except one pushed forward through the rest. A young man with a familiar face, one of his second-oldest sister's sons? Perhaps the second? The man cried out "uncle!" in Shanghainese.

~Jun?~ Cheng whispered to the air, but couldn't tell if any breeze carried the name for him.

The young man reached for Cheng, only to yelp and pull back with his face set in pain.

Cheng was too hot to touch. A bad sign, suggesting fire was growing too strong.

He apologized. Without words, all he could do was step back and bow with his hands together and his gaze fixed on his nephew.

An older Black woman hissed over the mark on Jun's skin. But Jun smiled, weak but genuine, at Cheng. He said something that Cheng didn't catch, then went on in Shanghainese, "it will be all right. I was just surprised."

Spiritless air rushed by Cheng as the woman who'd followed him ran around him—careful not to touch— straight into the arms of one of the strangers, babbling away.

So many people all speaking at once. At least his nephew was well, but otherwise the world was made of strange sounds and flickering flames underlying everything regardless of element.

The ghost stepped in front of Cheng and pointed at a man holding a circular stone glowing green.

~Take it,!~ she told the breezes, who told him. ~It will help you speak to the deep earth and keep your promise.~

Smoke rose from his skin and lightning continued to circle his head as he moved toward the other man, who stepped back.

Cheng asked a breeze to carry his words to Jun, so that his nephew might translate for him, but Jun showed no signs of hearing.

Then the ghost moved to stand next to a youngling, an air speaker with a distinct resemblance to the man holding the stone. A moment later, the youth said something to the stone-holder in a language Cheng didn't know.

The man held the stone out at arm's length.

Cheng cupped his hands beneath, and the man let the stone drop.

The weight knocked Cheng to his knees. He wasn't expecting the stone to be so dense and heavy. He gasped for breath, surprise having knocked air from his lungs.

And some of the fire and heat from his skin, for the stone was cool and smooth. Not a single point or rough line anywhere. The green shifted, lightening to that of new shoots pushing from the ground.

Water and earth had formed it. No hint of human working, human fixing, or human binding lurked in the rock, which came from far below the earth's surface.

So very different from the human-worked stones beneath Cheng's legs.

The earth's ongoing litany of safety and security resounded in Cheng's ears, this time with the kind of lilt his mother had used when she'd sung lullabies to Cheng and his sisters as children.

Cheng reached for the earth, but fire was in the way.

Why speak to the earth when he could speak to flame?

Later, Cheng promised, even if that would require flames that hurt him, but first he had a promise to keep.

Fire eased, for it understood promises.

Still the deep earth didn't hear Cheng.

Rather than taking the time to rise to his feet, he walked on his knees off the flagstone patio onto a broken mass of bushes and earth. Fire roused just enough to clear the brambles from beneath him, then subsided.

Cheng laid the glowing stone against soft dirt.

Startlement flared through him as the earth ceased its lullaby. Cheng's ears popped as his awareness of the world receded into the distance.

The ghost knelt opposite him, her silvery outlines overlapping with bushes and leaves. She spoke, and Cheng shared her sentiments with the earth.

~You gave us sanctuary from our pursuers. You shielded me from my husband's wrath. You cared for my family and gave us a home—but we no longer need this. Your protection has lasted long enough. Be as you were, and let me go.~

Glowing light appeared, connecting stone and spirit. With the deep earth listening and its reactions flowing through Cheng, he shivered at realization of what had happened. She'd somehow negotiated a binding with the deep earth that kept her spirit trapped in the world and unable to move on, because the deep earth moved so slowly it didn't recognize the shift from her life to her death and so held her here even as it continued to protect her earthly remains and the land.

~Let go?~ the deep earth asked.

Cheng shared this with the ghost, and she laid her hands on the stone. Silvery fingers became almost solid as the rest of her faded.

Light flared, running from palest green to the colors of decay.

Stones rumbled behind Cheng as the tomb collapsed, followed by cries and shouts as the others moved away from the pile of dust, bones, and decaying flesh.

~Fire send it back,~ earth said.

Cheng picked up the smooth stone, ghostly fingers clinging to the edges. His knees ached and he nearly tripped twice, but carried it across the patio to lay atop the rubble of the tomb. He waved at everyone to get back. Fire flared along his arms, giving his motions added effect.

Then moved back himself, to where he'd knelt before.

~Now?~ Fire asked.

~Now.~

The storm began to lumber over the land. The scattered breezes joined the immense wind propelling the clouds forward. Rain cascaded down, dampening everything but the flickers still running along Cheng's skin.

Cheng stretched his arms to either side. The small wisp of lightning that had wreathed his head jumped high into the air. A far greater bolt screamed down from the sky to strike the stone and tomb, turning all black. Thunder drove all sound from his head for a long moment.

More rains poured down on him, cooling without drowning. For once, Cheng didn't fear drowning in the water.

Healing seeped up from the earth, through the stones through his bare feet.

Winds twined around his arms.

His skin no longer crackled with fire, though the seed of fire remained within him much bigger than before.

He turned, ignoring all the people babbling questions in words he didn't understand.

"Wang Jun? Nephew?" he coughed, voice rusty and raspy, but the words came out clear enough for him to hear with his ears—and to reach Jun. Earth or fire or both—or all the elements—had somehow restored his voice and ability to communicate.

He swayed but before he collapsed, his nephew was there, holding him up and promising to take him home.

PART SEVEN
AUGUSTA DEYO

CHAPTER 29

MORE CHANGE

"Are you certain you won't stay a little longer?" Father asked as he guided Augusta through the busy train station.

"No." Augusta shook her head as they stopped several feet away from other clumps of passengers. She smoothed faint wrinkles from her jacket with trembling hands. She wore a new blue traveling outfit, a ready-made suit of new fabrics supposedly easy to care for, and a straw hat rested atop her head. Most of the clothes packed in her suitcase were carefully chosen for utility and practicality. Likewise, she'd been ruthless in deciding what items counted as necessities to pack versus what trinkets to leave behind. Only two photographs made the cut, one of her family before and the other a recent one of her father and brothers.

She set her feet to either side of the suitcase and laid her purse atop—a nicely large bag capable of containing food, drink, and more, and with a strong strap that she wrapped around her wrists.

Her surroundings barely registered, other than the general clamor of crowds waiting on the train, voices echoing oddly across the great expanse. It was neither cool nor hot, with all the bodies around countering the usual chill of morning, and the air redolent with all manner of food frying in oil. Her stomach rumbled, half in hunger for she hadn't managed any breakfast, and half in protest at the smells.

All the while her ticket rested in the breast pocket of her jacket, crisp and sharp-edged enough to slice a finger. It would take her only as far as Buffalo—Jake had purchased the ticket for her, and refused to make it for any farther just in case she changed her mind or decided to head south rather than west, which he allowed was more likely.

Her brothers had abandoned her to her father's company. Danny was off investigating the crowds and nooks and crannies of train station. Jake had gone with him, after exchanging meaningful glances with Father, though both would surely be back to help her on the train and say a last good-bye.

"We'll miss you." Father sighed. "There's plenty of work still to be done here, what with unraveling all the bindings George managed to lay on nearly everyone he met over the last years. New people with signs of being bound pop up nearly every day. There's a follower of that new field, psychology, who thinks it was a compulsion with him, not that that's likely to have any weight with the courts."

"You don't need me for that." Augusta untwined one hand from her purse strap to grab her father's hand. Just as well, since he also had to find a new way to care for speakers past the point of communicating with humans. He'd turned the Hall over to the Kanien'kehà:ka, who were busy addressing the damage George had caused. "You've all manner of Federal agents working with the Institute, and George and Quint locked up despite all their lawyers' pleas, with their major co-conspirators being turned up and nabbed."

"All the same, we'll miss you at home as much as at the Institute." He squeezed tight, staring at the flicker of light in the distance as the train rounded a curve and headed for the station. "And not just because you're one of the best unbinders anywhere, and I would know."

"You should. I learned most of it from you, and you know why you taught me," Augusta said. "And that's why I have to go."

"To find her?" He swallowed hard. "Them?"

"If I can, to say I'm sorry and to know how they are, or what happened to them. You're going ahead with having Mother declared dead." Her turn to swallow and glance away, the varied groups waiting for the train little more than masses of colored clothing. "I don't argue with that, but I need to go away so I don't follow in George's footsteps and bind us all to stay as we are. How much of the . . . lack of change at home since she left was my doing?"

He didn't answer at first, fingers stroking the back of her hand as he finally admitted, "I don't know."

"Neither do I." She pulled away and turned to face him straight on. Long horn blasts echoed through the air as the train slowed and puffed into the station. "That's one reason I want to leave, so by the time I do return, things will be different enough that I won't be tempted to make them as they were."

"I understand." He waited as she grabbed her purse, then picked up her suitcase. "And I hope you will understand if I have meddled just a little."

"What?" Augusta asked as he led her down the platform. Danny and Jake waved at them from further along.

"You only said you wanted to go south or west, no place

in specific yet, but somewhere that you might find work for a binder, though you have only to wire and I'll send money."

A situation Augusta hoped would never come to pass. She had her pay for the last years, and Father had already helped her hide coins and bills and valuables around her person and bags. He'd claimed it a father's privilege.

But he hadn't mentioned anything more, and the people near Jake and Danny were starting to look a little more familiar.

"So I made some arrangements, I would have liked for you to travel with Zhang and Wang, but they went south two days ago."

"So?" Augusta asked.

"Meet your new traveling companions." Her father introduced her to May and Luella Tobie.

Augusta had seen them both before, not least on the night Sanctuary Hall had ceased to be a sanctuary, but hardly spoken with either. May appeared calm and pleasant, tall and equitable in a traveling suit almost a match for Augusta's save having seen more wear.

Luella on the other hand, was likely the age Augusta had been when her mother left at best, or possibly younger, and didn't seem particularly impressed at the notion of traveling together.

Of course she was the one with magic, and a rare kind at that. Augusta had no doubt her father had arranged this for her benefit—but also in hopes that Augusta might pick up some information to funnel back to him.

"Your father says you're looking for family members. I don't find people." The younger woman lifted her chin and gave Augusta a square look. Beside her, May's lips quirked to the side in a half-smile.

"Did I ask you to find anyone?" Augusta asked. If the thought *had* crossed her mind, it was now thoroughly squashed.

Before Luella could reply, Augusta's father stepped in. "I accept that you do not take jobs to find people, but you can ease a father's heart by allowing my daughter to accompany you as she takes her first steps to find her path, and in return she can share with you what the Institute knows about pathwalkers."

In short, the reverse of what Augusta had guessed—or more likely both sides. Given how May's smile stretched wider as Luella blinked and took a second look, Augusta wondered if there might not be accommodations on both sides.

"I prefer finder to pathwalker." Luella nodded. "But we have a bargain."

"Ride with us a ways, and then we can decide," May offered, extending a hand.

Augusta shook it quickly as the train stopped. She hugged father and brothers, eyes smarting from tears she refused to shed just yet, and hustled on board with her belongings. Settled into a seat opposite her new companions, she watched her family and city disappear into the distance.

Her old life had broken beyond repair, but maybe she could make a new one that would suit her better. Time to find out.

The adventures continue! Sign up for Alea Henle's newsletter at https://BookHip.com/PCSWMCK *and be the first to learn when the next Finders & Binders book is available! (Bonus free short story set in her Dancing Princesses world.)*

About the Author

Alea Henle writes non-fiction by day and fiction by night. Contemporary and historical fantasy, fantasy romance—and more! Check out her website www.aleahenle.com.